The Strength to Endure

Royal Factions, Volume 6

W.J. May

Published by Dark Shadow Publishing, 2021.

This is a work of fiction. Similarities to real people, places, or events are entirely coincidental.

THE STRENGTH TO ENDURE

First edition. April 20, 2021.

Copyright © 2021 W.J. May.

Written by W.J. May.

Also by W.J. May

Bit-Lit Series
Lost Vampire
Cost of Blood
Price of Death

Blood Red Series
Courage Runs Red
The Night Watch
Marked by Courage
Forever Night
The Other Side of Fear
Blood Red Box Set Books #1-5

Daughters of Darkness: Victoria's Journey
Victoria
Huntress
Coveted (A Vampire & Paranormal Romance)
Twisted
Daughter of Darkness - Victoria - Box Set

Great Temptation Series
The Devil's Footsteps
Heaven's Command
Mortals Surrender

Hidden Secrets Saga
Seventh Mark - Part 1
Seventh Mark - Part 2
Marked By Destiny
Compelled
Fate's Intervention
Chosen Three
The Hidden Secrets Saga: The Complete Series

Kerrigan Chronicles
Stopping Time
A Passage of Time
Ticking Clock
Secrets in Time
Time in the City
Ultimate Future

Mending Magic Series
Lost Souls
Illusion of Power
Challenging the Dark

Castle of Power
Limits of Magic
Protectors of Light

Omega Queen Series
Discipline
Bravery
Courage
Conquer
Strength
Validation
Approval
Blessing
Balance

Paranormal Huntress Series
Never Look Back
Coven Master
Alpha's Permission
Blood Bonding
Oracle of Nightmares
Shadows in the Night
Paranormal Huntress BOX SET

Prophecy Series
Only the Beginning
White Winter
Secrets of Destiny

Revamped Series
Hidden
Banished
Converted

Royal Factions
The Price For Peace
The Cost for Surviving
The Punishment For Deception
Faking Perfection
The Most Cherished
The Strength to Endure

The Chronicles of Kerrigan
Rae of Hope
Dark Nebula
House of Cards
Royal Tea
Under Fire
End in Sight
Hidden Darkness
Twisted Together
Mark of Fate
Strength & Power
Last One Standing
Rae of Light
The Chronicles of Kerrigan Box Set Books # 1 - 6

The Chronicles of Kerrigan: Gabriel
Living in the Past
Present For Today
Staring at the Future

The Chronicles of Kerrigan Prequel
Christmas Before the Magic
Question the Darkness
Into the Darkness
Fight the Darkness
Alone in the Darkness
Lost in Darkness
The Chronicles of Kerrigan Prequel Series Books #1-3

The Chronicles of Kerrigan Sequel
A Matter of Time
Time Piece
Second Chance
Glitch in Time
Our Time
Precious Time

The Hidden Secrets Saga
Seventh Mark (part 1 & 2)

The Kerrigan Kids
School of Potential
Myths & Magic
Kith & Kin
Playing With Power
Line of Ancestry
Descent of Hope
Illusion of Shadows
Frozen by the Future
Guilt Of My Past
Demise of Magic
The Kerrigan Kids Box Set Books #1-3

The Queen's Alpha Series
Eternal
Everlasting
Unceasing
Evermore
Forever
Boundless
Prophecy
Protected
Foretelling
Revelation
Betrayal
Resolved
The Queen's Alpha Box Set

Watch for more at www.wjmaybooks.com.

THE STRENGTH TO ENDURE

By W.J. May

Have You Read the C.o.K Series?

The Chronicles of Kerrigan
Book I - *Rae of Hope* is FREE!

BOOK TRAILER:

http://www.youtube.com/watch?v=gILAwXxx8MU

How hard do you have to shake the family tree to find the truth about the past?

Fifteen year-old Rae Kerrigan never really knew her family's history. Her mother and father died when she was young and it is only when she accepts a scholarship to the prestigious Guilder Boarding School in England that a mysterious family secret is revealed.

Will the sins of the father be the sins of the daughter?

As Rae struggles with new friends, a new school and a star-struck forbidden love, she must also face the ultimate challenge: receive a tattoo on her sixteenth birthday with specific powers that may bind her to an unspeakable darkness. It's up to Rae to undo the dark evil in her family's past and have a ray of hope for her future.

Find W.J. May

Website:
https://www.wjmaybooks.com
Facebook:
https://www.facebook.com/pages/Author-WJ-May-FAN-PAGE/
141170442608149
Newsletter:
SIGN UP FOR W.J. May's Newsletter to find out about new releases,
updates, cover reveals and even freebies!
http://eepurl.com/97aYf

Royal Factions

The Price for Peace – Book 1
The Cost for Surviving – Book 2
The Punishment for Deception – Book 3
Faking Perfection – Book 4
The Most Cherished – Book 5
The Strength to Endure – Book 6

The Strength to Endure Blurb

THERE'S ONLY SO LONG you can hold back the tide...

With the weight of a kingdom behind her, Elise is ready to go back to where it all began...but who will be waiting when she arrives?

Old secrets come to light as a horrible truth is finally revealed. Friendships shatter and strain as each of the friends is called upon to make that final sacrifice.

The players are ready. The stage is set.

But who will be standing when the dust finally clears?

Chapter 1

It had been three days since the shipwreck. Three days since that fateful storm.

Not an exceptionally long span of time, but I was having trouble remembering anything that had happened before. The desert had a way of doing that to you. Of burning memories away.

"Come on, you're doing great!" Will called, glancing back at the scattered line of people behind him. "Let's pick up the pace a little—try to get to that next bluff."

I felt sorry for him.

Ever since we'd trekked away from the beach, marching across the scorching plains towards his childhood home, he'd made it his personal mission to keep spirits high. It was a noble effort, but there was a lot that was working against him. The terrain, for one thing. His friends, for another.

And there was no escaping that relentless sun.

"I don't understand," Zadie panted, staggering along beside me. "Your people grow crops, Will. How can you do that if there's no water?"

"There is water," he answered, helping Jane over an outcropping of rocks. "But it's rationed by the capital. Where I come from, the thing people most often die from is the heat."

We shot him a dark look.

Sometimes, the biggest thing working against Will was himself.

He played back the words, bit his lip apologetically, then gestured us forward with a huge encouraging smile. "That's it, everyone! Just a little bit farther! No one's going to die..."

His voice trailed away near the end as we hitched our bags higher and continued over the endless plain. It wasn't a desert the way I'd imagined as a child. There were no cacti, no camels, no rolling hills of sand. The ground was hard, cracked—so completely devoid of nourishment that it was a wonder the entire place didn't crumble right off the map.

Will assured me his home didn't look like this. The land there had been irrigated, different colors stretching across the landscape in quilted patterns of violets and greens.

It sounded beautiful.

But we were nowhere near his home. And even if we managed to get there, there was no escaping the suffocating, baking heat. An ironic shift from Nimoa, where everything was water.

Water.

My stomach twisted and my desiccated mouth throbbed just thinking the word. In a fevered daze, I remembered how Will's first thought when washing ashore was to find water. We should have listened. But when we'd caught sight of another ship drifting out at sea, bearing the colors of the royal army, we'd left the beach in a panic and headed further inland. We'd taken whatever supplies had washed to shore with us, but there hadn't been time to scavenge for much—and there hadn't been much there to begin with. The biggest slap in the face was a pair of empty canteens.

In Midlark, the cold was far more likely to kill you. The village was right by a river, and that river was always brimming with the newly melted snow. We never had to worry about dehydration.

My body didn't understand how to cope with it now.

"I don't understand how you know where you're going," I murmured, gaze roving across the plains. "Everything here looks exactly the same."

There was a strange, ragged quality to my voice that startled me. Just as startling was how much effort it took to speak. Will gave me a quick look, then called again to the others.

"That's it, everyone—let's get a move on! Who wants to race me up that next hill?"

A FEW HOURS LATER, a small miracle happened. We found a dried-up stream.

At first, I thought it was another slap in the face. That the gods of irony were having a bit of fun. But Will's entire face transformed the second he saw it. Without a second thought, he grabbed a walking stick from one of the sailors and began digging with all his might.

"Help me," he panted, waving Remy forward. "You're good at this. You grew up in a mine."

Remy simply stared at him before turning to one of the other men from Reeves.

"Is he crazy, then? Has the sun driven him mad?"

The man smiled weakly, but hopped down into the dusty channel and started digging right alongside. A few minutes later, the ground darkened. A few minutes after that, we found the stream.

"That's incredible!" Zadie gasped in astonishment.

"There isn't much," Will cautioned, grabbing one of the canteens. When he pressed it to the ground, a tiny trickle of water flowed over the lid. "But we can make it last."

For the next few hours, that's exactly what we did.

We worked until the sun went down, digging and shifting and kneading the ground, until we had enough water to fill both canteens. At that point, we promptly collapsed and decided to set up camp right there in the dried-out streambed. It wasn't like there was much to prepare. There were no tents, or blankets, or coverings of any kind. If there had been, we'd use them only for shade.

"That's it, sweetheart. You can drink a little more."

Will and I glanced over to where Demetrius was holding the lip of the canteen to Ella's eager mouth. She slurped furiously, reaching for it again when the sailor eased it away.

"The rest is for you," he said apologetically.

Demetrius shook his head, giving it again to his daughter.

"She can take mine. Just a few more gulps, honey." He stroked her dusty hair. "Then we need to give it to someone else, okay?"

It was a heartbreaking sight, but Will pushed reluctantly to his feet—dismissing the sailor with a discreet nod as he knelt by their side.

"You need to drink some yourself," he said quietly, tickling Ella's feet. "You won't be any good to her if you're too weak to stand."

"I need you to show me the best place to dig," he countered, keeping the canteen firmly to his daughter's mouth. "When she goes to sleep, I can try to find some more."

Will sighed, raking back his hair. "Demetrius, you mustn't—"

"Will," he interrupted sharply, but said the words with a smile, "talk to me again when you have children. Now show me where to dig."

The evening passed very slowly after that.

The grueling day had left us exhausted, but the heat made it impossible to rest. For what felt like hours, we tossed and turned. Trying to find a way to get comfortable, wondering what kinds of animals prowled the plains, before the moon rose high in the heavens and sleep finally took us.

"KEEP VERY STILL...UNLESS you wish to die."

My eyes shot open to see Isabelle hovering over me with a fierce expression. She had a knife in one hand and a rock in the other. For a horrified moment, I thought she meant to solidify her claim on Will by ending my life forever. Then I saw the tiny green lizard perched on my leg.

"Oh, it's adorable—"

"Damnit, Midlark!"

The creature sprang away as the blade plunged into the ground just an inch away from my kneecap. I leapt back with a gasp but she had already ripped it back out, glaring the whole time.

"I was *trying* to catch some breakfast!"

"And here I thought you'd finally made a friend."

She lifted the knife again, but Will eased gently between us—pulling me backwards whilst flashing her an innocent smile. "Morning, Izzy. Did you sleep well?"

Her fingers tightened on the grip before she stalked in the opposite direction, muttering under her breath about reptiles and unrequited love.

"You know, I was thinking," I murmured, watching her storm out of the creek, "maybe we could try to leave her in Reeves." Will shot me a quick grin, and I lifted my hands. "I don't mean tied up or anything. I just meant with a nice family...in a good home..."

He chuckled quietly, leaning back on his arms. "Not sure how many good homes you're going to find in Reeves."

I flashed him a look. "You had one."

His smile stilled for a moment before fading ever so slightly. "Yes, I did."

We were quiet for a while, watching as the same sailor from the night before picked up the remaining canteen and began moving from person to person. After a while, Will lifted his arm and slipped it over my shoulder. It was too hot for such things, but I leaned into him all the same.

"Are you nervous to go back?" I asked softly. "To your township, I mean."

The last time he'd been there, a crowd of his childhood companions had watched as he was dragged off his land by a pair of royal soldiers and thrown in the back of a truck. The last time he'd been there, his little sister had been alive—screaming at the window for him to come back.

He shifted uncomfortably, then dropped his arm.

"Does it matter?" he asked stiffly. "It was one of the largest in the province, at a central hub for shipping and trade. Plus, I know a few people. It makes sense that we would go there."

I watched him discreetly, then scooted a bit closer.

"That isn't what I meant," I murmured, tracing my fingers along the delicate bones in his hand. "You said that it was one of the biggest, but surely there are others. If you don't want to go back, I'm sure we can..."

I trailed off at the look on his face.

He wasn't staring at me, but somewhere just behind me. I twisted around to see the sailor with the canteen patting Remy on the shoulder before walking away.

Will was on his feet a second later, intercepting the man on his rounds.

"Why didn't you give some to Remy?" he asked bluntly.

The sailor glanced over his shoulder before shaking his head.

"I offered...but he declined."

I pushed to my feet as well, staring in confusion as the sailor took Will by the elbow, lowering his voice with a gentle tone. "It's a brave thing, what he's doing. Don't press him."

Brave?

Remy didn't look brave. He looked sick.

His eyes were red and deeply shadowed, while his lovely face was tinted a worrisome shade of grey. Both legs were sprawled, though there was a strange delicacy to the way he was holding himself. But more pressingly, those bruises he'd gotten in the shipwreck weren't beginning to fade. If anything, they looked even worse—shadowing like trouble-some clouds over his fair skin.

I'm an idiot.

I hadn't realize how bad things had gotten, but all the clues were there. He'd scarcely helped with the funerals. He hadn't dug for water like the rest. This from a man who wouldn't lie down until everyone else was safely settled. A man who'd been trained since childhood not to complain.

He glanced up when he saw us coming, forcing a weak smile.

"Are you ready for another day of hiking?" he teased, mimicking Will's tone. "Your attempts at optimism are getting almost—"

Will shoved the canteen in his face.

"—painful."

There was a beat of silence.

"Drink."

Remy let out a sigh, as though it was an effort just to speak.

"I shouldn't," he said softly.

"*You shouldn't?*" Will echoed incredulously, giving it a shake. "What are you—"

"Look at me."

"I don't know what you're—"

"*Look* at me," Remy repeated patiently. "I saw injuries like this all the time back home, when there were cave-ins or falls. Either you get better, or you don't. I'm not getting better."

While most of us had been tossed about during the storm, emerging with a variety of broken bones and torn skin, Remy had been crushed the very moment he'd stepped off the stairs.

I had vague memories of one of the lifeboats flying towards him, pinning him against a wall.

"That is ridiculous," Will said stiffly. "You're hurt, not dying. I won't allow you to speak like that, and I won't allow you to hasten the process along. You're going to *drink*, Remy. *Now.*"

Remy smiled at him fondly, leaning back against a rock. "I'll stay with you as long as I can, but don't waste that water on me."

Will's eyes flashed as he gave the canteen another violent shake. At this point, I wouldn't have been at all surprised if he'd wrenched open Remy's mouth and poured it down his throat.

He gritted his teeth, trying to rein in his temper. "I'm not asking—"

"And I've made up my mind."

"Remy—"

"Your tone is outrageous."

"Damnit! Take the bloody—"

"Tell me you don't speak to Elise this way."

"Are you joking about this?" Will said dangerously, eyebrows raised to his hair. "You've essentially sentenced yourself to *death*, and you're making jokes—"

"Let him be," the sailor interrupted gently.

Will turned around slowly, refocusing all that rage. "Excuse me?"

The man flushed but held his gaze. He had over twenty years of age and experience on both teenagers, and he knew a lost cause when he saw one. He also happened to have a son.

"You heard what he said...and he's right. We need to save this for people who can—"

"You don't know him," Will snarled, hands curling into fists. "It must be very easy to say such things, when *you don't even know his bloody name*!"

The sailor's eyes flashed—tempers were wearing thin. "You didn't know most of our people," he countered. "People we lost in the storm whilst delivering your message—"

"It's everyone's message, you were heading down the coast anyway, and we buried your friends all the same! Now, you are going to help me give him a *bloody* drink!"

"Break it up," Isabelle said tiredly, trudging towards us from further down the bank. She took one look at what was happening then slipped her hand into Will's. "We'll be back soon."

He took an automatic step towards her, then paused. "Wait...what?"

My eyes shot between them as Remy pursed his lips.

"I'm going to help you calm down," she said innocently. "...*sexually.*"

Will stood a moment in baffled silence, then he screamed into his hands. The others hastily averted their eyes. There was a chance he might have finally broken. But he resurfaced with a grin.

"Why did we take you along?" he demanded.

She closed her eyes, pulling in a long breath. "I'm so glad you're finally asking yourself that question."

The tension broke as the sailor walked away, chuckling. I watched him go before picking up the second canteen and taking the dagger from Isabelle's hand.

With a sweet smile, I knelt in front of Remy.

"Pick one."

NEEDLESS TO SAY, THE day got off to a rough start.

Remy was finally convinced to take the water (mostly because, while I wouldn't cut him it turned out that Zadie would), but in spite of Demetrius digging for almost half the night, the stream bed was dry and there wasn't any more to be found.

"That's all right," Will said bravely, trying to bolster spirits as we left the camp behind and started trekking across the rocky plains. "I guarantee that isn't the only stream out here. We'll find another before you know it. We can even scout up ahead for some more."

"Yes, we can," the sailor agreed.

The two men looked at each other, then nodded silently. The argument was forgotten as they drifted in opposite directions, helping the others hobble forward in a line.

If it was possible, the sun was even hotter that morning than the day before. It wasn't long before we were sweating, removing any clothes that weren't absolutely necessary and wrapping the damp fabric around our heads. In desperation a small group of people hurried onward, scouting ahead for other sources of water while the rest of us limped weakly along.

"Do you have any idea how far it might be?" I croaked, inhaling a mouthful of dust.

Will shook his head, keeping a constant hand on Remy.

"I never travelled beyond the township. If the captain hadn't said the first port was on the border of Reeves, I wouldn't have even known where to start."

Remy shot him a fleeting look. "...your pep-talks need some work."

I snorted with laughter, while Will offered a cheerful smile.

"Oh, I'm sorry...you had hoped to be dead already. Would you like me to walk you back? I know there's at least one lizard running around to keep you company—"

"We found something!"

The entire group of us froze in unison. After a full day of bodies washing up on the shore, those words had lost their charm. We squinted into the distance as one of the sailors waved his arm.

"Come on—we've found something!"

Zadie shook her head involuntarily. "We've got to stop using that phrase..."

The rest of us stood there, unwilling to commit. If they hadn't been standing the way we were already headed, there was a chance we would have simply gone around.

"It'll be fine," Will chanted as we trudged forward, mumbling under his breath. "There's nothing out here but the group of us. It'll be fine."

But on at least one point, he was dead wrong. As soon as we cleared the top of the bluff, we realized there was something else out in the desert. But it was the last thing I'd ever expect.

It was a truck. And behind the truck...was a road.

Chapter 2

"It's a trap."

It was hard not to see Isabelle's point. Standing in the middle of the desert, with five gulps of dirty water in our stomachs, it was hard to trust in the miraculous appearance of a truck.

The keys were still in the ignition. The road looked unnaturally clean.

But we gathered around it despite our misgivings. Somehow, just the proximity was enough to lift spirits. A truck was an escape. A road was a guarantee there were other places in the world besides this wretched desert. I didn't care about the keys. I was on the verge of kissing it.

"It's a trap," she said again. "We should give it a wide berth. See if there are any tracks in the sand. Clues that might tell us—"

"It's not a trap," Will said quietly.

The rest of us turned to him in unison, like some breathless congregation, too nervous to hope, while Isabelle threw up her hands in exasperation. He shook his head, abnormally calm.

"We were shipwrecked, washed ashore, then travelled the next four days in a zig-zag pattern across the desert." He shook his head again, staring at the truck. "They couldn't have controlled any of that. They couldn't have predicted it. This isn't a trap."

We were quiet a moment. Then Zadie looked back the way we came.

"...we've been zig-zagging?"

"It isn't a trap," he said again, resting a tentative hand upon the door. "When I was growing up, there were cars and trucks all over Reeves. Food's not some static commodity, it will spoil. They had to transport it quickly. This kind of thing was always lying around...and this used to be a road."

Used to be...what happened to it?

"Why would they just leave it?" Remy murmured, unconvinced. His voice was dangerously weak and his eyes were in constant danger of closing. "Where did the driver go?"

"Probably scouting for irrigation channels." Will circled the vehicle, picking up speed. "They were always looking for ways to expand. He probably just hopped in with someone else, and didn't even remember he'd left it. I'm telling you...this is not an unusual sight."

The idea alone was baffling, but my concerns ran deeper.

"It's not an unusual sight," I repeated cautiously, "but you're not getting inside. Why not?"

His cheeks flushed beneath the scorching sun. "Of course I am," he mumbled. "I'm getting in right now."

After a few inexplicable false starts, he opened the door and climbed carefully into the driver's seat. Both hands came down slowly, as if deviating from some pre-rehearsed routine, and he glanced reflexively in the rear- view mirror, though we knew there was no one for miles.

Zadie stared at him incredulously, then clapped her hands.

"Great job, Will. You look like you're selling cars." With an impatient gesture, she jabbed a finger at the controls. "Does it work?"

He followed her gaze...and shrugged.

William was subsequently strangled by his friends.

"Honey?" I began sweetly, throwing the others a quick glance. "Why don't you turn the key and give it a try?"

He startled like I'd said something impossible, then went inexplicably pale. "I'm sure there's not gas—"

Demetrius flipped a door shut, giving us a thumbs-up.

"I'm sure it won't start—"

Zadie reached past him and turned the key.

The engine roared to life.

"Well, that's just..." He gripped the steering wheel, looking like there was a good possibility he might throw up. "That's just...unexpected."

I took a step closer, hissing under my breath.

"Why are you being so strange? This could *save* us—"

"We're not allowed."

There was a beat of silence.

...excuse me?

His cheeks burned scarlet as a ringing silence fell over the desert. Most people were staring in complete bewilderment, but Remy stepped forward with a little smile.

"What was that?" he asked innocently.

Will blushed again, but seemed physically incapable of lifting his hands to the wheel. The engine alone was enough to send him into a mild panic attack. He sank an inch lower in the seat.

"...we're not allowed to drive the trucks."

For a split second, our problems vanished and I found myself holding back a smile.

Old habits die hard, and the some of the lessons ingrained in us since childhood were notoriously difficult to shake. There were certain actions whose reprisals were so unimaginably fierce, you could simply never fathom yourself doing them. Even if the people who'd punish you were nowhere in sight. Even if you and your friends were technically roasting to death in the sun.

"William," Remy said with everlasting patience, "you understand that we're organizing a *rebellion* against the capital? Some people have already died—"

"Yes, I know," Will said irritably, steeling himself with a breath.

In an act of sheer bravery, he tapped ever so lightly on the gas. The truck inched forward and a thrill of adrenaline washed over him, like a kid 'borrowing' his father's hatchet for the first time. He cast another

involuntary look over his shoulder, then waved us forward with a boy-
ish grin.

"Hop in...we're going for a ride!"

The rest of our companions clambered dutifully into the back, while Remy and I lingered on the edges with the same amused look. The transformation was remarkable. Instead of freezing rigid in the seat, as if waiting for the sting of a whip, Will was slouched as low down as he could manage, stretching out his long legs whilst casting occasional looks at his reflection in the rearview mirror.

"How long do you think he's waited to say those words?" I murmured.

Remy shook his head with a grin. "I think he's forgotten that he doesn't know how to drive..."

THE NEXT FEW HOURS were...*interesting*, to say the least.

You'd think it would have been relatively easy to navigate such a vehicle, given that there was nothing but miles of flat, shapeless earth as far as the eye could see. You wouldn't necessarily think the truck would manage to find every divot, bounce over every pile of rocks, knock loose one of its tires to avoid what turned out to be a shadow, whilst joyriding in the sun.

You would have been wrong.

"This is unbearable," Demetrius hissed, passing off his daughter before reaching up towards the front. "Stop the truck, we're trading places."

Zadie glanced over at him, looking distinctly impressed. "You can drive?"

"I can't possibly be any worse than this." Demetrius kicked the back of the driver's seat as the truck lurched forward. "*Now*, William!"

It cannot be overstated how much I *loved* that his full name was catching on.

"Just give me a few more minutes," Will pleaded, inching forward to avoid the reach of his hands. "I'm getting the hang of it, I swear. Just a few more minutes, then we can switch."

"If my daughter has even a *single* bruise—"

"She was in a shipwreck, Demetrius."

"One single bruise—"

Their voices faded to an angry clamor as I stared out the window, resting my chin on the frame. The only good thing that had come from our impromptu jaunt through the desert plains was that we were in the desert no longer. The tawny browns and burnt yellows had given way to a rolling blanket of green that stretched from one horizon to another. Even with the wind whipping my hair I could feel the moisture all around us, seeping up from the ground. Even if the truck were to self-detonate in protest and we had to continue by foot, I was sure that by digging alongside one of those emerald seams we could find enough water to keep us going.

If nothing else, it might get us out of the bloody truck.

"It's a little romantic, right?"

I glanced over in disbelief as Will reached out to take my hand. Despite the trail of carnage we were leaving behind us, he was positively beaming—infused with his own abominable light.

There was another violent lurch, and I opened my mouth with a choice response before Zadie nudged me discreetly in the ribs. We were dating. This meant that, on occasion, we had to lie.

"...very romantic."

Ironically, one of the sailors who'd teased us about motion sickness took that moment to lean as far out of the truck as was possible, his face tinged a delicate shade of green.

"I'm going to throw up."

NOT LONG AFTER, THERE was a groan of protest from somewhere deep in the engine. The truck began to slow down before giving up the ghost entirely and rolling to a gradual stop.

There was an audible sigh of relief.

"Thank the maker." Isabelle hurled her body out of the truck before falling to the ground with a gentle kiss. "I'll never do it again. I promise."

The others chuckled quietly, then began extracting themselves from the metal frame. Leaping to the ground, one after another. Many were making similar vows to the heavens, others had simply resolved to murder Will in his sleep.

Remy tried to swing his leg over the side, then slumped back in exhaustion. His chest was rising with shallow, uneven breaths, but no matter what he did, he wasn't getting enough air.

I climbed immediately into the truck, kneeling beside him. "What can I do?"

"Nothing," he panted, shifting himself higher. "There's nothing to be done." He lifted a trembling hand to his chest before falling back with a grimace. "I wasn't lying, what I said to Will. There is no fixing something like this. In Bunkhill, we used to call it the long death."

I shot him a secret look before gently draping his arm around my neck.

"More and more, that's just sounding like a dreary place." Moving as gingerly as possible I helped him stand, shuffling alongside him to the edge. "It's my opinion that we shouldn't visit. They can sit out the rebellion in the mine."

He laughed painfully, gripping the side of my neck.

"You'd better hope that Joseph took his group there first. Unless you want half a ton of explosives falling into enemy hands..."

We stopped at the edge of the truck, gauged the distance down, and didn't see a way it would be possible. Before he could say anything else, I waved for Will.

"A little help?"

He jogged over immediately, positioning himself with a wicked grin. "Fall into my arms, princess."

Remy took a step back. "I'd honestly rather die."

"Be sensible—" I chided.

"Would. Rather. Die."

"Kneel down, Will," Demetrius suggest lightly. "Then he can step on your head."

There was an instant chorus of assent from the rest of them as Will glanced over his shoulder with a look of betrayal. By the time he turned back, Remy had warmed to the idea.

"I'm okay with that."

Of course you are.

"This is ridiculous," Will muttered, sinking to his knees. "Like I really believe you're saying that for Remy's benefit. This is about the—"

"This is about the truck," Demetrius finished bluntly.

There was a resounding chorus of applause as Remy stepped theatrically down from the truck, using his friend as a stepstool whilst waving to the crowd. The only mercy was that he stepped on Will's shoulder instead of his head. But to be honest, I think he was simply afraid to fall.

"Thanks, buddy." He lifted a bracing hand to his ribs, but still managed a smile. "You're right, we should do that more often—"

"That's a seed barrow!"

I glanced down in surprise as Jane shoved past me, throwing herself to the ground in front of a rudimentary piece of equipment half-buried in the field. It seemed to be little more than a toothed plank attached to a giant wheel. It was overturned and rusted, clearly forgotten for a long time. But her face lit up as she ran her hands over the surface, eyes dancing with excitement.

"Uh...yeah," Will answered with a hint of confusion. "We used to fix them up every year after harvest before the capital finally sent us something new." He paused a moment, looking her over with a frown. "How did you possibly know that?"

She never took her eyes off the machine.

"I read about them." Her fingers curved around the metal before she glanced hopefully over her shoulder. "Can we take it with us?"

...what?

The rest of us exchanged a look. The thing was huge, well over a hundred pounds, and had been discarded by some of the most practical people in the kingdom for having no value.

"Not this time," I said gently, helping her back to her feet. "But I'm sure where we're going, you're going to see a lot more of that sort of thing. Right, Will?"

"Yeah, definitely." He flashed her a quick smile before glancing towards the hills. "And I actually think we're getting close...I recognize that skyline."

FOR THE NEXT TWO HOURS, we marched over the fields with renewed energy. Perhaps it was the thrill of finding something familiar, perhaps we were simply grateful to be out of the truck. Far more likely, we were desperate to find a way out of the punishing sun.

"I don't know how you did it," I panted, wiping my forehead as Will and I paused to let the others catch up. "You'd work in the fields from morning to night? I'd pass out the first day. You'd find me lying amongst the turnips."

He laughed quietly, lifting a hand to shade his face.

"Then you'd be whipped," he said simply. "The soldiers were always very generous with the whippings when I was growing up. Sometimes they would pull someone out of the line and whip them for no reason, just to show the others what would happen if they were to fail."

I shivered involuntarily, trying not to imagine it.

My village had been too small to warrant a royal presence, but I had seen glimpses of such things at the palace. The images were burned into my mind. Yet when Will had been whipped after our failed escape, the threats made against his sister had hurt him infinitely more.

"Do you..." I trailed off, hesitant to continue, "do you want to visit your house while we're here? Surely there are some things you must want to see." I paused again at the look on his face. "If nothing else, just to pick up some clothes—"

"No," he said shortly.

The conversation dropped quickly as the others joined us on the sloping trail.

It was clearly defined now. Not a faint path through the greenery, but something that had been cut and smoothed. As we continued in silence, I couldn't help but imagine a childhood version of the man I loved scampering gleefully beside me—the wind in his hair, the sun on his cheeks.

Three brothers, he'd had. Along with a little sister. As we rounded the side of one of those rolling hills, I realized I'd never even asked their ages. I didn't even know their names—

There was a soft gasp and Will stopped abruptly, staring over the bluff.

In the valley below us, a twinkling settlement stretched from one side of the green to another; smaller than a city, but larger than a town. It was cushioned on every side by a patchwork of endless fields—all connected by little pathways, with canals for irrigation in between. The houses were modest, but comfortable. Every few miles, the community widened into a center square.

It was...picturesque. There was no better word for it. *Far* too hot for my tastes, but lovely all the same. The only thing that marred the picture was a row of metal barracks on the edge.

"How many soldiers?" Remy asked quietly, coming to stand beside us.

After a few seconds of silence, I glanced expectantly at Will. But the man was momentarily lost to the rest of us, staring as though in a trance, with those distant lights flickering in his eyes.

Only one other man from Reeves had survived the shipwreck. He had gone silent as well, staring down into the valley with the same faraway look in his eyes.

"Will," I nudged him gently, "the soldiers?"

"Hmm?" He turned to see us watching, and quickly composed himself. "Oh, there aren't many this time of year. They'll come back in full force later in the spring, when it's time to plant."

His eyes swept over the settlement again, zeroing in on one particular spot.

"We should...uh...we should probably find a place to camp for the night," he said vaguely, hands clenching by his sides. "Come up with a plan for the morning..."

I shared a quick glance with Remy, then took one of those rigid hands in my own.

"Sure, that's a good idea," I said with deliberate calm. "From this distance, we can probably just see where those soldiers are headed and intercept townsfolk on the opposite side. If there are actually as few as you say, we could even—"

But Will was already leaving, abruptly moving towards the valley.

"That sounds good, Elise," he called over his shoulder. "Whatever you think is best. I'm just going to...I just need to check something..."

Just like that, he was gone.

My mouth fell open in shock as I froze where he'd left me. The rest of the group was in a similar state of shock, watching as his silhouette got smaller and smaller in the distance.

It took a few seconds to recover my senses, then I bolted after him with a tight smile.

"It's all right!" I called, stumbling over the rocks. "Just set up right here. We'll be back before you know it! This is all part of the—"

My boot caught on a rock and I came down hard, inhaling a mouthful of grass.

"—plan!"

"WILL!"

I raced along behind him, trying to keep up with his long strides. For the last twenty minutes, I'd been trying to catch up. But while I was tripping over every dip and ridge in what had been falsely advertised as a 'flat' land, it was like he was charmed.

With an almost eerie grace, he floated along in front of me—arms hanging straight by his sides, eyes never leaving a specific point that always seemed a ways in front of him.

"William!"

Again I stumbled into the underbrush, emerging with a crooked twig lodged in my hair. I yanked it out with a glare, cursing under my breath as my fingers came away covered in sap.

"Would you STOP!" I hissed, tearing after him once again. *"Look, I know this has to be terrible, but you're not thinking clearly! But you're going to walk straight into some royal guard—"*

My nose crunched as I smashed full-force into his back. The sun was vanishing behind the hills, and in the dusky light I hadn't seen when he stopped right in front of me.

I circled around quickly, but his eyes weren't on me.

They were staring, without blinking, at a house not far in the distance. One with an overgrown walkway and shingles missing on the side of the roof.

There was another house not far away from it. One that looked in far better repair. A small group of people was gathered outside, but I didn't see the uniform of the guards. That fact alone was the only thing that kept me from grabbing his cloak and dragging him right back into the hills.

Not that I could have moved him. Never had I seen such an expression on his face.

"Honey," I lifted a tentative hand to his back, staring with him, "...is that your home?"

His eyes were shining, but there weren't any tears. For how long he must have imagined coming back, there was a strange sort of disconnect in the way he was looking now.

After a few seconds, he shook his head.

"It isn't my home," he breathed. "There's nothing left."

What could you say to such a thing? In a way, he was right. The place was nothing but memories now. Memories so haunting, it was nothing more than a tomb.

Another minute passed, then I gently pulled him away.

"Come on," I said softly. "We need to return to the others—"

A tiny voice spoke up from behind.

"Will?"

I knew who she was before he even told me. Before I'd even whirled around and registered the presence of a child. There was no mistaking those dark eyes.

This was Will's sister.

Claudie was alive.

Chapter 3

She flew to him with a force that defied her size, knocking him backwards with the intensity of it. For a split second Will was too stunned to move, then his hands lowered slowly.

"I'm dreaming," he breathed, clutching her tiny head. "This can't be real."

Tears filled my eyes, but I didn't dare move a muscle. There was a faint commotion on the other side of the shared yard as a group of people ventured tentatively from the other house.

"William?"

I lifted my head as a tall woman stepped towards us. She was shaped like some of the instruments they had lying around the palace. Wide hips, rounded curves, and a long, slender neck.

"Is that really you?"

Will spared her only the quickest glance, but his thoughts were consumed with his sister. A kind of fever had come over him, flushing his skin though his face was white with shock. He held her tighter for a moment then knelt down slowly to the same height, holding on to her tiny wrists.

"I thought..." He shook his head, unable to complete a sentence. "They told me you had..."

While he was reeling, Claudie looked as though she'd come back to life. A beaming smile lit those elfin features, and when he started to weep she wiped the tears from his face.

"Don't cry, Will." She wrapped her arms around his neck, squeezing tightly. "You're home."

As if the sight of her face wasn't enough, the sound of her voice overwhelmed him. For a few silent minutes, he simply held her and cried. Smoothing back her wavy locks, reassuring himself again and again that the nightmare was over—that his little sister was actually alive.

When at last he was able to compose himself he stood up slowly, lifting her at the same time. The neighbors, who I was assuming was the family he'd hoped would take care of her, had been keeping a respectful distance, but gathered suddenly closer, still bursting with surprise.

"I was told she'd been killed," he murmured to the woman, unable to stop trailing his fingers through her hair. "The commander of the army told me himself...that she'd died months ago."

A belated shudder ran through my shoulders. I remembered the moment well.

We'd been in the garden, the commander and I. He'd been in the process of tearing off my dress, when Will had appeared from nowhere and saved me. As a reward the man had toyed with him most cruelly, throwing the death of the little girl in his face.

Many things had changed since then. But Will had never been quite the same.

"It was nothing of the sort." The woman squeezed his shoulder, eyes crinkling with a warm smile. "We weren't going to let her starve. She moved in the day they took you away."

His eyes flashed again to her face, lingering longer this time. "But the queen's soldiers—"

"They came," she interrupted, looking suddenly strained. "They searched your house." The tension cleared when she looked at the other children. "We told them she was our daughter."

I was stunned.

They say that a hard life makes for hard people. I wasn't sure I quite believed that, but there were limits to neighborly compassion—of this I was sure. The penalty for knowingly misleading the queen's guards was death. Not just for this kind woman, but for her entire family. That she would be willing to take such a risk? All for the sake of one orphaned child? I couldn't comprehend it.

Will looked so utterly astonished, the woman actually smiled. She squeezed him again before gesturing to the girl's dark hair. "It wasn't hard, Will. She even looks like one of ours."

All at once, I realized this was true. In the time we'd been talking, the rest of her family had discreetly gathered around. All of them were colored the same way—with tan skin and dark locks.

Will noticed them at the same time and tried to smile. There was clearly history there, but he was clutching the body of his resurrected sister and was quite simply overwhelmed.

"They showed me her notebook," he said suddenly, turning again to the woman. He seemed almost afraid to address Claudie directly, like if he tried to look at her straight-on she might simply disappear. "The queen was holding one of her notebooks."

A whispered hush swept over the others, and it occurred to me how fantastical those words must sound. Their childhood friend had gone to the capital. He had spoken with the queen.

Even the mother was shaken though she recovered herself quickly, gesturing to one of the younger boys. "Silas was always trying to steal them, so Claudie kept them at your house. I think it was her way of keeping things normal, of keeping you alive..."

A strange look came over her face, one that said she had been just as worried about him. No one knew quite what became of the people brought to the palace, only that none of them ever came back. She could hope that he'd simply married and remained at court, but anyone who had known him personally knew it was far more likely that he'd been executed trying to escape.

"And now you're here," she concluded.

The ringing silence that followed weighed heavy with the question, but I still wasn't sure if Will noticed. It wasn't until I took a step closer that he focused suddenly.

"Miranda...what news have you heard from the palace?"

She straightened up a little, not expecting the question.

"We hear nothing all the way out here, you know that." She paused a moment then continued in a rush, unable to contain her curiosity. "Were you claimed, Will? Or did you displease them in some way? I don't wish to upset you, it's just...I've never heard of anyone coming back."

Did we displease them? You could say that.

"It's a bit of a story," he said slowly, glancing backwards at me. "And we're hardly the only ones to tell it. The sun is setting soon. Perhaps we could continue speaking inside?"

I WENT BACK ALONE TO get the others. It wasn't a hard journey, just a few minutes hiking back into the hills, and for the moment Will was physically incapable of letting go of his sister. I had only gotten halfway before I found the rest of them—already worried and coming to find us.

They were delighted by the news about Claudie—especially Zadie and Remy, those who had known his story and grieved with him in silence. They were slightly more hesitant to venture into the open without first accounting for the soldiers, but the moment we returned to the pair of houses all those fears were laid to rest.

Never had I met more hospitable people than Miranda Stonege and her family. Never had I been so warmly beckoned into a stranger's house. There was scarcely enough room to fit all of us, but somehow we managed to fit. Then we managed to settle down. Then we told her our story.

There were some major edits. There were children present, after all, and whenever we came to a subject too volatile Will should shake his head sharply and glance at his sister. She was still sitting in his lap, but had twisted around to stare with wide eyes at whoever was speaking.

I couldn't blame her. In spite of all the edits, the tale was a shock.

We flitted from one person to the next, filling in each other's sentences, trading off as though we'd rehearsed it. When at last we were finished, a long silence filled the little house.

"So you've come here to see who will join you?" Miranda asked slowly. The oldest of her sons leapt to his feet, pledging instant support, but she waved him down without looking, keeping her eyes on the rest of us. "Is that why you're here, Will?"

He tightened his grip on Claudie, quiet but sincere.

"I'm here to offer people a chance. It's no longer question of starting a rebellion, the people of Nimoa took care of that. War is coming and Reeves is right in the middle of it. When the soldiers come, you can submit as you've always done...or you can fight back."

Miranda gave no reaction.

"But not here."

I leaned forward, speaking for the first time.

"No, not here. When the fight happens, it will be at the capital. Only by tearing down those gates can we finish what we've started. But the people of Reeves can help in other ways."

She shook her head, gesturing to her children. "How? You see what life is like here. We are a people of families, not warriors. What skill can we possibly leverage against such things?"

Zadie caught her eye with a little smile.

"When it comes time to send your crops to the capital...perhaps you could get confused?"

There was a moment of silence. Then a ripple of laughter flooded the house. Even Miranda had to join in near the end, shaking her head indulgently.

"This is your plan? To starve the beast?"

Will grinned with the rest of them, then shrugged as though such things were inevitable.

"Our crops are usually carried to the capital aboard the train, but my friends and I have already taken care of that. The soldiers will then be forced to come for them by ship, but the people of Nimoa have the strength and numbers to refuse them. That leaves only the roads—which spread across the entire realm. If we can send food to other provinces, they will trade supplies in return."

Her son was standing again, pushing a mop of dark curls from his eyes.

"And what of those of us who wish to fight?" he challenged, puffing out his chest. A proud dusting of hair graced the bottom of his chin. He couldn't have been more than twelve years old.

Miranda's face grew fierce, but Will smiled again—shaking his head.

"I task you with feeding not the capital, but the *entire realm*. And still you imagine you'll have time for more? Besides, who will protect your mother if you're gone? What of your family?"

The boy threw a sideways look at his siblings, then sank reluctantly back in his chair.

"You're only a few years older than I am," he muttered.

"And somehow I find myself impossibly in your debt." Will pushed to his feet as the others began talking amongst themselves, crossing the room and offering his hand. "You helped to care for my little sister when I was away. That was very brave, Luke. You have my thanks."

The boy startled in surprise at being addressed in such a way, then took Will's hand with a blushing smile. The two shook firmly before Will returned to my side.

"You know, he didn't really take care of me," Claudie whispered as the room began to empty. Most people had decided to make camp on the other side of the hill until we'd decided what to do with the soldiers in the morning. "A few weeks ago, *I* actually warned *him* about a snake."

Will scooped her up once again, kissing those rosy cheeks. "A snake? Was it huge?"

"Don't make fun," she said seriously. "It was tiny, curled up in his shoe."

He threw back his head with a laugh I'd never heard. One that was both infectious and utterly relaxed. One that made me drift closer with a secret smile.

Claudie spotted me immediately, leaning towards him again.

"She's very pretty," she whispered.

I looked down with a blush as Will glanced over his shoulder. The blush amused him, and he squeezed his sister with a little grin. "She is, isn't she? Pretty enough for me, do you think?"

Claudie shook her head with a giggle. "Far too pretty for you. She could do much better."

"Finally, someone agrees with me!" Zadie sashayed towards us with a coaxing smile, Remy trailing along after her. "So this must be the famous Claudia. Your brother speaks of nothing else."

"We're very glad to meet you," Remy added kindly.

We're very glad to see you alive.

The little girl smiled shyly in return, holding tight to her brother. But the second Remy had spoken, Miranda stepped forward with a look of alarm.

"My dear boy, are you all right?"

It was clear that he wasn't, but before he could say a word she snapped her fingers and a small boy raced to her side.

"Silas, go and fetch Old Lady Hatterley. Be quick, now."

A dark head of curls sailed through the door, even as Remy shook his head.

"That's not necessary—"

"She's a healer," Will interrupted quietly, taking his arm. "Saved me from the fever when I was just six. The woman can work miracles, Remy. Let her take a look at you."

Remy set his jaw stiffly, bracing against the pain. "It's a waste of time—"

"Then *waste* the time."

A tense silence fell between them before Zadie slipped in between and took Remy firmly by the arm. "Let's just wait for her outside, shall we?"

He acquiesced with a quiet sigh, and followed her towards the door.

Please, let that work...

Miranda stared after them with a look of motherly concern, watching as they disappeared into the darkness before murmuring under her breath.

"An explosion, a shipwreck...it's a miracle you came back alive."

Will's eyes snapped up, filled with some uncertain emotion. Then he tugged me discreetly on the sleeve. "That jewel you got from the wedding dress...do you still have it?"

I glanced up in surprise as he grimaced a silent apology.

"I would do anything to get you another," he breathed. "But my *sister—*"

"No—of course!" I replied immediately, rummaging around in my robes. Having sewn the tiny gem inside the satin lining, it was one of the few things to have survived the shipwreck. In a perfect world, we would save it for some future use. But past debts must be paid first.

I ripped through the stitching with my nail and pressed it into his hand. He flashed me a grateful smile, but didn't look twice before turning and presenting it to Miranda.

"I can never repay you for what you've done," he said quietly, head bowed in gratitude. "But perhaps this can be a start."

It took her a moment to register what she was seeing. Then her mouth flew open in shock.

"William, what did you...?" She reached to touch it, as if verifying it was real, before her arm dropped back to her side. "I can't take something like this!"

"You must," he insisted. "It's all I have to give you."

"It's worth more than half the township!"

"Then this is money well spent."

She stared back in complete bewilderment before shaking her head with a fond smile. "How many times did you help my family after Saul died? How many times did you put food on my table? Did you ask for money when you saved Luke from drowning in the canal? We help each other, Will. That's what our people do—"

"This goes beyond that," he interrupted softly, unable to look her in the eyes. "You didn't think I was ever coming back. You were prepared to take her for life. I can't..." His throat tightened and he shook his head, pushing it back into her hands. "*Please*—take it."

"And what would I do with such a thing?" she teased, eyes twinkling affectionately. "Do you think in addition to farming potatoes, I'm a notorious ruby-smuggler on the side?"

That stopped him.

"Then...take the farm."

That stopped *her*.

"What?"

"My family's farm," he answered slowly, as if the idea was just coming to him. "There's no one left to run it. I'm giving it to you. The house as well," he added suddenly. "I'll sign it over on paper, make it official in case anyone happens to ask."

"Are you sure?" Claudie whispered.

Are you sure?

"But that's..." Miranda trailed off in amazement. "Where will you go, Will?"

There was a moment when he looked as baffled by the question himself. But the moment passed quickly, replaced with the light of adventure, the quickest flash of a secret smile.

"I'm not sure yet." His eyes twinkled as they met mine. "Maybe somewhere by the sea..."

Chapter 4

Will and I slept away from each other that night, for the first time since leaving the palace.

It wasn't particularly planned. In fact, I'm sure I would have been welcome to stay in his childhood home, but the man needed time with his sister. I returned with a smile to the camp.

Most everyone was already settled down. Only Jane had abandoned the rest and was crouched on the edge of a field, endlessly fascinated with the discarded farming equipment.

"Is that safe?" I asked Demetrius under my breath, staring down from the adjacent hilltop as he scattered the remains of the fire. "To wander so freely in the open?"

He glanced up once before shaking his head.

"Of course it isn't safe. But there isn't anyone for miles, and even if there were I doubt they could see her in this light." He paused a moment, almost guilty. "There's also a chance she wasn't quite listening when I asked her to return to the camp."

Something in his voice made me smile.

"Wasn't quite listening?" I repeated curiously.

There was another pause.

"...she was singing."

I swallowed my laughter and patted him on the shoulder, setting off down the hill to recover her myself. He was right about the lighting, we'd spoken to Will's neighbors until well after dusk. The sun was nothing more than a smoldering memory on a distant horizon as I made my way carefully down the grassy slope, until it leveled out in a field of rich, loosely-turned dirt.

Jane was on her knees, running her hands over a twisted piece of metal.

"This is most wonderful," she murmured, eyes racing back and forth as though still reading the lines from her book. "Exactly the way it was pictured."

I crouched down beside her, without the faintest idea what I was looking at. "What's it called?"

"It's a hay rake," she muttered like a mad scientist, running her fingers over the wheels, "but it's been repurposed to better handle the terrain. You see the added spring section here?"

I turned to her instead, warming with a little smile.

"You read about these?" I asked. "How?"

Jane and I might have existed in slightly different dimensions, but we had come from the same place. We didn't have any books on farming in the village. The library boasted a total of five novels—three of which were so heavily scribbled upon it was impossible to make out the text.

There had been no gap between Midlark and the time we spent at the capital. Yet she spoke with the authority of one who'd learned such things firsthand.

"When I first got to the palace, Eric let me use his library."

I stopped cold, like someone had dug a razor into my skin.

There were maybe six people in the world who would dare call him by that name. Two were dead. The others were amassing armies to destroy one another. And there was Jane.

"...he did?"

I scarcely recognized my own voice. The field tilted suddenly, and I felt faint.

"He was an interesting person," she murmured, almost as if she'd forgotten as I was there. It was the way she processed things, I realized. In summaries.

Interesting. The same way Matthew was smart.

"He thought it was interesting that I wanted to be a farmer," she added suddenly.

My head snapped up like it was on a string, still trying to picture this odd, inaccessible girl in his private study, browsing the many shelves of his library. I had marveled at them myself, staring in silence as he and the countess played cards. The two images were impossible to reconcile.

The land around us was dark, with few stars to light it, but I stared intently into those bright, curious eyes. "You spoke of such things?"

She nodded lightly, still touching the machine.

"On occasion." A nail curved suddenly down the side, making the metal sing. "It's such a beautiful profession, don't you think? Water, earth, and sunlight. If properly cared for...things will grow. It is a perfect simplicity. I would like very much to try."

I stared at her in silence. My mother had always thought farming to be noble—food was vital, they were helping people survive. But I didn't think such a thing would matter to Jane, if it had occurred to her at all. The challenge was in the growth. The crops were of little consequence.

"And Eric...he agreed with you?"

She tilted her head, considering.

"He saw the appeal," she finally answered. "After all, war is simplistic as well, is it not? And Eric's business is war." She returned to the machine with a shrug. "Or at least it was."

She left a moment later, standing abruptly and making her way back up the hill. I was left staring at the broken machine behind her, kneeling in the fragrant ground, trying to catch my breath.

I kept myself deliberately awake until morning. I couldn't risk any dreams that night.

"YOU LOOK TERRIBLE."

Splinters of blinding sunlight forced their way into my eyes as a silhouette shadowed the sky above me. An impatient foot kicked at my side, jostling me back to life.

"...Zadie?"

The shadow smiled, revealing a row of pearly teeth.

"Get up—we're going to check on Remy."

I sat up slowly, gingerly, still marveling at the intense heat of the sun so early in the day. It had just barely risen over the eastern hills, but already the air in the little valley was boiling.

"He didn't come back last night?" I asked, pulling on my shoes.

She shook her head, sweeping her long crimson hair off her neck and into a high ponytail.

"No, that old woman wanted to keep him. She seemed nice enough, but there was a number of questionable-looking things hanging in her cottage. There's a chance she's a witch."

She said each sentence in the same even tone—oblivious when I paused in surprise, staring at the back of her head. A few seconds passed, then I couldn't help but smile.

That's Zadie.

A few years after I was born, a craze of witchcraft had swept through the realm. No one really took it seriously, though we'd all come to fear the repercussions if such an accusation were ever made. In retrospect, it was easy to see the palace had used such things as a way to execute dissidents. Either that, or it was merely to isolate the population even further—flaming suspicions between neighboring provinces. The craze soon faded, though the lexicon remained. A rather silly yet surprisingly effective plan, given that no one actually believed in such creatures.

"Oh yes?" I teased. "What sorts of things?"

"Carcasses, crystals, a map of bones arranged to look like the night sky."

...maybe she's a witch.

"And you left him there?" I accused, following her down a trail that ran along the base of hill. A few scattered houses were nestled in the grass beside us, shutters closed tight.

"I couldn't get away fast enough," she said without a hint of shame. "It's doubtful that he'll forgive me, but hopefully he won't remember. He was in pretty bad shape…"

She trailed off as we reached the end of the path, only to find Remy himself. He was sitting on the porch of what could best be described as a hovel, with the exact woman about whom we'd just been speaking. Whether she boasted unholy powers or not, he didn't seem to mind. In fact, the two seemed to have struck a kind of accord. He was leaning against the wall with a rather peaceful look on his face, both hands lifted as she used them to wrap a seemingly unending coil of twine.

…which she uses for hexes and spells…

She didn't look up at our approach, but Remy lifted his head with a smile.

"Good morning."

I froze in amazement. It certainly was!

Gone was ragged weakness to his voice, and gone was that sickly pallor. It had been replaced with his usual lovely shine. The bruises remained, but even they had begun changing—reversing their dark course and lightening around the edges with shades of purple and blue.

"I can't believe it," I gasped, unable to help myself. "She…she cured you."

The woman looked up at his, but only to give him a wry grin. Some silent message passed between and he laughed under his breath, never lowering those obedient hands.

"She saved me," he clarified. "But I'm far from cured."

Zadie hovered at the edge of the porch, afraid to get closer.

"But how?" she asked in astonishment. "How did she do it?"

It was clear now that her casual abduction of me that morning had been nothing more than a front. She'd been afraid to come back on her own, terrified as to what she might find.

He grimaced in spite of himself. "Very painfully."

With a permissive glance, he slipped the twine from his hands and pushed delicately to his feet. Almost immediately a thin crimson line appeared on the side of his shirt, but the woman didn't appear concerned. She merely smiled as he kissed her lightly on the cheek, then waved in farewell.

The three of us headed back towards the houses, at a slow and easy pace.

"I didn't even thank her," I remarked incredulously, when we were far enough away. "The woman saved your life, and I didn't say a word. I never even got her name."

Remy glanced over his shoulder with a faint smile. "Her name is Hazel. And she prefers the quiet—the woman's mute."

Zadie turned to him with wide eyes. "Wait—really? Then how did you learn her name?"

"I divined it," he replied simply. When she and I froze with the same gaping expression, he chuckled under his breath. "You're both jumpy this morning. She wrote it in the dirt."

Oh. Right.

Zadie shot me a meaningful look, as if this peculiarity was par for the course. In case that wasn't enough, she cleared her throat importantly. "Elise thinks she's probably a witch."

"I never said that!" I cried indignantly. "*You* said that! On account of the vermin and bones!"

"Quiet," she hissed. "I'm sure she can still hear you!"

Remy laughed again, ushering us down the path. "Aren't you supposed to be more enlightened than all that?" he teased. "Born of the mighty merchant class? That sort of nonsense is for uncultured hicks like Elise."

I nodded sagely. "Or little rat-people like Remy, burrowing away in the ground."

He laughed again, lifting a bracing hand to his side. "We had troubles enough in the mines, but I'm fairly certain there were no witches. If there were, they had a depressingly practical way of doing things."

We paused outside Will's house, staring up from the lawn.

"He stayed the night with his sister?" he asked softly.

I nodded, eyes on the house. "He's still in shock. Keeps trying to convince himself that she's alive."

We were silent a moment, then Zadie lit up with a grin.

"I'll go wake them up! I'm getting really good at that!"

She left before we could stop her, no doubt planning her own dark sorcery as she threw a dramatic wink over her shoulder and slipped inside. I grinned in spite of myself, hoping she kept the violence to a minimum, before casting a glance at the handsome man standing by my side.

"I've seen injuries like yours as well," I said quietly, suddenly unable to look at him. "Remy, I truly didn't think you would survive."

Since we'd washed ashore, I'd diligently pretended otherwise. It had been surprisingly easy to do so, this from a girl baptized in harsh realities and cold truths. Perhaps it was just that the person in question was too precious. It would break me to imagine anything different. He was beside me today, he'd be beside me tomorrow. Only on the day that he wasn't would I face that kind of pain.

He bowed his head with a sigh.

"Neither did I," he said quietly. "Dozens of people died each year from such a thing. You learned to recognize the signs. The soldiers always said it couldn't be fixed—threw some fancy medical jargon at us. But after what happened last night..."

His eyes flashed and a cold anger settled on his face.

"It's not some incurable condition. None of those people had to die. It takes some skill, some time. It takes a little damn effort—" He sucked in a quick breath, but never lost that chilling calm. "Our lives weren't worth the food rations it would take to help us recover."

There were those harsh realities again, slapping us in the face. Only this time we didn't turn away. We'd been taught not to. We'd been taught to face them head-on.

"So you're in this."

He laughed harshly, eyes on the distant sky.

"Till the bitter end."

Chapter 5

Whatever Zadie had done to rouse the others had left a lasting impression. By the time we stepped inside, Claudie was still giggling and Will had flushed with a seething rage.

His entire expression changed when he saw us, stilling with breathless surprise.

"You're all right!"

The relief betrayed the worry of the night before. No matter how much faith he had in the old woman, no matter how many times he'd crept in secret to peer through her window in the dark, a part of him had been convinced it was one of his friend's last nights on earth.

Remy smiled weakly, glancing down at himself. "So it would seem."

In a second, Will swept across the room—kissing me swiftly on the cheek before gently manhandling his friend into a chair at the kitchen table. From there he was a flurry of motion, pushing the chair closer to the wood, clearing a space, needlessly adjusting the angle.

I realized with a smile, the layer of nerves behind each gesture. For the first time since being dragged by force into the finery of the palace, Will was hosting someone in his own home.

"Let me get you some breakfast," he offered effusively.

Remy nodded, looking a little overwhelmed. "Okay."

Will beamed in response, then went instantly pale—raking his fingers through his hair with a slightly manic expression. That tension tripled as he glanced towards the bare cupboards, layered in dust and hanging ajar from lack of use. He stared a moment, then glanced quickly at his sister.

"Claudie, do we have any—"

She burst out laughing before he could finish the sentence, perched in what seemed her usual position atop a high cushioned stool. "Of course not! No one's lived here for months!"

The rest of us graciously hid our smiles, while he ground his teeth together in frustration.

"Well, could you go next door—"

"I'll go with you," Zadie said quickly, probably in a casual attempt to avoid his rage. Her eyes danced with a victorious smirk as she slipped past him. "Sorry about earlier. Honest mistake."

A muscle twitched in his jaw, but he only smiled as the two girls vanished outside. When they were gone, however, he turned back to us with a serious, almost regretful expression.

"I'm afraid the redhead has to die."

Remy and I laughed at the same time, shattering any tension that remained in the room. Will took a final look at the barren cupboards, then slumped into a chair at the table in defeat.

I alone remained standing, staring around the room with quiet curiosity.

Because the house itself consisted of a single room—its various purposes delineated only by the pieces of furniture. The boys were sitting in the 'kitchen', because that's the section that had the table. I was standing in the living room, because it was accented with a long and narrow couch. At the far end, I could see a single bed that Will and Claudie had shared the night before.

Three brothers...along with their parents. Where did everyone else sleep?

There were a few personal touches—a stack of worn books, a child's lantern, a little wooden truck that looked like it had been passed through a dozen sets of tiny hands—but they had been hoarded into a single corner and draped with an old blanket.

I wondered if this had been Claudie.

Since throwing herself into her brother's arms, the girl had been permanently attached. Her spindly arms locked around his neck, her dark head of hair rested in the hollow of his neck. She'd left the notebooks he'd given her as a remembrance—that's what Miranda had said. I could easily imagine her wandering back to the house in secret, taking out his old things, playing by herself. I could just as easily have imagined him playing as a child. I wished I could see the titles of the books. I wondered if I'd read anything like them myself.

"So this is your house," I murmured. *Was* his house. I kept forgetting he'd given it away. His cheeks colored ever so faintly, and I was quick to add, "It's much bigger than where I grew up."

It was meant to make him feel better, but it also happened to be true. The cottage may have been sparse, but it was large. My own home could probably have fit twice inside it.

"It's bigger than where I grew up as well," Remy added, playing idly with the table. His face was still pale but his eyes were bright and curious, jumping from thing to thing.

Will nodded distractedly, glancing around. "Most people who live here have large families. We're encouraged to have large families," he added suddenly. "The more children, the greater the workforce. They used to give incentives..."

He shook his head, unwilling to say more.

"Children don't live long in the mines," Remy said thoughtfully, eyes still flickering about the house. "I never had any siblings...I always wondered what that would be like."

Harder, probably.

I turned around to study him, curious such things hadn't come up before. "So it was just you and your parents?"

He hesitated a split second.

"It was me and my mother," he said simply, and left it at that.

This wasn't uncommon. I was sorry to have asked. Especially because my own situation was exactly the same. With a forced smile, I perched between them on the windowsill.

"It was just me and my mother as well."

Both of us spoke in the past tense without really intending to. It was hard to do anything else. Our time in the palace had a way of erasing everything that had come before. We clung to each other now. We clung to the present. It was hard to reconcile images of the past.

"I didn't know that," Will said quietly, his gaze upon my face.

He seemed a bit uncertain, as if he wished the two of us were alone. But just as he opened his mouth to speak again, the door burst open and a dozen or so children rushed inside.

They were all different in looks and age, but united by those features that marked everyone who lived in such a place. Bare feet, windswept locks, and skin that had been darkened by the sun.

I pushed to my feet in alarm, but Remy grabbed my wrist with a quick hand.

"We all have secrets, Elise, and now it's time you learned one of Will's." He gestured to the menagerie with a little smile. "He is their father—"

"Stop that at once!" Will smacked him with a grin as the children burst into laughter all around us, little faces full with light. "What the heck's the matter with you?!"

"I almost died," Remy said unapologetically. "It changed me."

A burst of breathless laughter escaped my lips as my heart slowed to its usual pace. But the children remained a mystery. They were circled around us now in a little crescent, eyeing us with just as much interest as we were looking at them. For a split second I thought they must have heard the rumor of our arrival and snuck off to see for themselves, but it appeared they were expected.

"You got here fast," Will remarked, pushing to his feet.

The tallest of the bunch nodded swiftly, still grinning ear to ear.

"Right after breakfast," he blurted. "My mother spoke with Miranda. Everyone on the strip is talking about the stories you told of the palace. Or rather...how you *left* the palace."

It was clear he wished to speak for the rest of the group, but almost immediately a tiny girl stepped in front of him, staring up at the three of us with enormous blue eyes.

"Is it true what they say, Will?" she whispered, torn between terror and excitement so extreme the combination had frozen her in place. "Did you really meet the queen?"

"Was she wicked?" another boy exclaimed before he could answer. "Was she as terrible as all the stories say?"

Will held up a silencing hand.

"She was wicked," he said softly. "She was terrible." He paused a moment, looking them over with a very serious expression. "And it isn't enough that they're speaking of it on the strip. This is a story that needs to travel. Do you understand what I'm saying?"

They nodded in unison, like a flock of solemn birds.

"It must only be heard by the right kind of people," he continued cautiously, driving the point home. "People who might help it spread."

By now there wasn't a child in the kitchen who wasn't poised on the tips of their toes, bursting with anticipation at the chance to prove themselves. He continued speaking quietly as I glanced at Remy—who looked as puzzled as me. By the time I looked back, it was already over.

"If there is any trouble," he concluded slowly, "any trouble at all...you simply turn around and walk away." His face grew still and serious as I'd ever seen. "I need your word on that."

The children nodded again with unnatural synchronicity, eyes bright with anticipation and that ever-present need to prove. Many were already angling towards the door, intent upon their sworn mission, but the older boy spoke up again.

"But we mustn't give up so easily," he argued. "If we see any buzzards, we can just—"

"You *walk away*," Will repeated sternly. "Swear to me, Henry."

There was a pause.

"All right, I swear."

The others murmured their agreement, then swept out of the house as though blown by a strong wind, scattering in opposite directions, vanishing just as suddenly as they'd appeared. I stared in fascination out the window; their feet didn't even leave prints in the dust.

That's our plan? A flock of little messengers?

"Buzzards?" Remy asked curiously.

Will glanced over in surprise, as if he'd forgotten we were still there, then shook his head dismissively. "It's what the children here call the soldiers. If you see enough of them circling, someone's probably dead."

I shuddered at the visual, pushing it deliberately away.

"And the strip?" I asked instead.

"Did you see the canals that divide this valley from the hilltop?" he asked, watching as we nodded in reply. "Each neighborhood is divided into strips. Miranda was able to spread our news to everyone in this community easily enough, but there are many others. It might sound foolish, but children are actually the best way to deliver such a message. They move quickly and are able to slip from one place to another without being noticed by the guards."

It didn't sound foolish at all. Quite the contrary, there was a chance it might actually work.

"Like a little flock of birds..." Remy murmured.

I flashed a faint smile.

"I was thinking the exact same thing." My eyes strayed again to the window, imagining I could see tiny figures darting amongst the fields. "So what exactly are they going to say?"

Will leaned back, stretching his long legs beneath the table.

"The same thing we told to those in Nimoa—that we aim to starve the capital of supplies whilst rallying an army to march against it. We'll offer them a choice. To help or to remain."

"And what of the soldiers that are already here?" Remy asked with a frown. "Should we—"

Will shook his head quickly, interrupting the line of thought.

"No, Miranda is right. This is a land of families, not warriors. When the trucks come for the crops, they will be our trucks. Full of our people. They'll deal with the soldiers. Until then, the people here will carry on exactly as before."

His confidence was catching, but so many factors were out of our control. Would the people here decide to help? Would the people in other provinces send those trucks? If a single thread were to pull too far, it seemed our entire master plan could unravel on the spot.

We all felt the weight of such things, but chose to speak of immediate concerns instead.

"And what of those who wish to fight?" Remy asked softly. "We're trying to raise an army, but they have no place to go. We can't march separately upon the capital—we go together or we die."

At that point Will openly hesitated, developing a sudden preoccupation with the table. Once or twice, his dark eyes flashed apprehensively to mine before he answered in an innocent tone.

"I told them the same thing I told Jasper back in Nimoa. You remember where the train was loaded, the abandoned station at the base of the eastern mountains?"

We nodded again and he lifted his shoulders in a casual shrug.

"No one from the provinces has ever really travelled. It would be impossible to find a rallying point that everyone knows. But everyone who's been to the palace knows that station."

It took a second for it to click.

"By Midlark," I stated in surprise. "You're talking about Midlark."

It shocked me, then it didn't. He was right about the need for a rallying point. He was even right about the train station being the one place besides the capital itself that everyone in the realm would know. But the proximity was suspicious, as was his tone.

"Not specifically," he said quickly.

Remy glanced between us with a hidden smile.

"Seems that way..."

"The woman who helped you is a witch," Will muttered under his breath. "Keep talking, and I'll see that she hexes you for sport—"

"William."

His eyes flashed again to mine, bright with secret nerves.

"It's *not* about Midlark," he said again, kicking Remy preemptively under the table. "It's about proximity. You were the last to be picked up by the trucks, you had the shortest distance to get to the train. Those mountains stretch all the way to the entrance of the capital..." His line of thought trailed off, as he was consumed again with the table. "The fact that it happens to be near your home...?"

I didn't know whether to be amused, touched, or exasperated. Unlike anyone I'd ever met, Will had a tendency to elicit each of those feelings at the same time. I glanced at Remy for support but the threat of witchcraft seemed to have subdued him, leaving me on my own.

"The village itself is still hours away by truck," Will continued quickly, "high in the peaks themselves. I'm sure there won't be the slightest opportunity to return."

I nodded slowly, eyes lit with a scathing grin.

"And if we happen to be the first group to arrive?" I tilted my head to the side, mimicking his innocent tone. "If there are weeks before the others manage to join us?"

He opened his mouth uncertainly, plotting some innocuous reply, then brightened with obvious relief as the door opened behind me with Zadie and Claudie's return.

"Oh, look—breakfast!"

WE ATE BREAKFAST QUICKLY—A simple porridge very similar to the kinds of meals I'd grown up eating at home. Then Remy and

Zadie returned to share what had happened with the rest of our group, and Will headed next door to work out the logistics of the farm with Miranda.

Claudie and I were left alone, washing dishes in the sink.

For a long time, the two of us worked in silence—shooting each other secret glances paired with shy smiles. A few times I opened my mouth to speak, but the little girl was so nervous I held my tongue each time. It wasn't until we'd run out of dishes and water that she finally broke down.

"Was it really so terrible?" she blurted suddenly. "Back at the palace?"

I stilled in surprise, then set down the towel I was holding. Of all the things for her to be wondering, it was perhaps the most obvious. Yet the question still caught me by surprise.

"It doesn't make sense, does it?" I replied, sinking down onto the sofa. "Hot meals, gardens, a place to sleep. An actual *palace*. It doesn't make sense for it to be terrible."

She perched on the cushion beside me, hanging on every word.

"I remember the first time I saw it, when the train cleared the trees. I could hardly catch my breath. It was *so* beautiful. Jewels glittering in the frames of the windows, flowers climbing over everything, towers that stretched all the way to the sky."

I shook my head, remembering those first few moments. There had hardly been a need for guards to escort us, as the instant they set eyes upon it every single captive was stunned. There was no escaping the might of it. No way to avert one's gaze. No way to avoid feeling small in comparison.

...which I suppose was the point.

"But it wasn't the palace that was terrible. It was the people inside it."

She considered this a moment then hung her head, staring down at her hands.

"Will won't tell me what happened," she admitted. "Not what *really* happened. Silas said he was probably beaten...but I don't know what it means to be claimed."

I stiffened involuntarily, the word sounded strange in that chirping little voice. If Will hadn't told her the specifics, it certainly wasn't my place to do so. But I understood the girl had questions. I would have had questions myself.

"They made him think you were gone," I said quietly. "Could you imagine if someone had done the same thing to you? There's nothing more terrible than that."

She nodded in silence, eyes flitting to the toys stacked in the corner.

"Is that why you burned it down?"

Come. Home. Now.

I flashed a quick glance at the house next door, praying for a rescue, but when none came I scooted closer to the girl on the couch. Her cheeks were still rounded with youth, always on the verge of a smile, but I could see each of the tiny bones running along her wrist.

"Have you ever gone to sleep hungry, Claudie?" I asked, already knowing the answer. "Have you ever closed your eyes, knowing there probably wouldn't be food tomorrow as well?"

She looked up at me, then nodded.

"Well, the people in the palace never go hungry. They have so much extra food they end up throwing it away at the end of each night." I nudged her gently, my leg next to hers. "They're meant to be responsible for people like you and me. They're meant to take care of us. But instead they hide away in that beautiful palace, throwing away food while the rest of the realm starves."

In a flash, Theo's face drifted through my mind. That look of innocent supplication as he stared at the plate in front of him, asking to send it home instead.

"That's why we burned it down," I said quietly. "Because no person should have so much if they're unwilling to share it with the others. No person should have the right to take your brother away from you, to stop so many others from ever coming back."

It was quiet for a while. Without thinking about it, she was leaning against my arm—eyes dancing with a thousand secret thoughts as her legs swung lightly from the couch.

After a few minutes, she peered up at me.

"So...you picked my brother over the prince?"

I caught my breath, torn between a denial and a grin. She made it sound so simple. In a way, I supposed it was. In the end, I just shrugged my shoulders in a helpless sort of way.

"That doesn't make sense either, does it?"

"No," she giggled before glancing up with a shy smile, "but I'm glad you did."

WE WEREN'T ABLE TO spend much time in Reeves. Despite it being the 'off-season', as Will called it, there were still plenty of soldiers stationed in the valley and we couldn't press our luck. Just a few days after arriving, it was already time to leave. We took the last afternoon for ourselves.

"So how did Claudie take it?"

Will and I had stolen away from the rest of the group and were walking along a pathway deep in the plains. The sun was hanging stubbornly over the crest of the hills, refusing to set but painting the sky in a brilliant array of colors. Twisting auburns and stunning golds. It was remarkably peaceful, especially considering the shouting match that had dominated the hours before.

"I can't tell if you're being sarcastic," he answered, eyes on the hills. "Did you hear us?"

I fought back a smile, wandering alongside.

"I'm not sure there's anyone left in realm who *didn't* hear you."

He'd been putting off the conversation since we arrived—battling with himself over the question of whether his little sister would continue traveling with us, or stay behind in Reeves.

He had some strong thoughts on the matter. As it turned out, so did she.

"It isn't the same with Demetrius and Ella," he said with exasperation, as if they were still arguing back and forth in the kitchen. "That child is *known* by the palace. For all we know, her mother is still alive. They will be looking for her. But Claudie isn't at any risk unless—"

"I know," I interrupted gently. "I heard you say it."

Several thousand times.

The little girl hadn't understood why another child would be allowed to accompany us, but she would be made to stay behind. No matter what her brother had said to convince her, she would see his decision as nothing more than abandonment and betrayal. She had made that quite clear.

"She won't forgive me." He paused suddenly, as if to catch his breath. "Not ever, not for something like this. If I leave her again...she'll hate me for the rest of time."

My head bowed in silence.

I knew that it haunted him—the image of her little face in the window, screaming as the soldiers took him away. There were nights when he'd wake up suddenly, pale and lost for breath. Times when I'd catch him gazing into the distance and I knew it was her face blazing in his mind. The thought of doing such a thing again, this time willingly, was almost too much to bear. There was a moment amidst all her begging and pleading when I thought he might actually stay.

"Everything is forever when you're six years old," I said softly. "If you'd asked me at that age, I would have sworn I wanted to spend eternity as a pony. But the eastern valley is no place for a child. In time, she will understand this. For now, you are her protector. You must decide."

He pulled in a breath, nodding a little as his eyes swept once more over the distant line of the hills. There were a hundred rises and curves, and he knew every one of them.

After a long time, he glanced back. "You wanted to be a pony?"

Silence.

"Really latched on to those salient details, did you?" I smacked his chest as he chuckled, then waved my hands impatiently. "Why exactly did you bring me out here to this pile of dirt?"

It was *exactly* the right question to ask.

"To show you this!" Without further ado, he leapt atop a hollowed tree trunk—lifting his arms in triumph. "Here it is. This is the place I hid for two days after running away from my house the first time. My older brother found me, dragged me back by the hair."

I stared incredulously, then burst out laughing. Time had worn away all evidence, but in my mind I could still see the defiant grooves in the dirt left by his nails.

"It's also where I had my first kiss, read my first book." He stepped from one side to the other, gazing out towards a dip in the hills. "If I'd ever dreamed of being a pony, I most certainly would have done that here as well. This was my spot. I came here almost every day."

His hand lowered and I took it, stepping up with him.

"First kiss, huh? Some illiterate farmhand I'm sure—"

"Maisy Dewhurst," he replied promptly. "The most beautiful girl I've ever seen, present company excluded. We decided to get married shortly after—the priest wouldn't do it on account of us being five. A few years later, she decided to marry my brother instead. Bit of a traitor, I suppose."

I laughed in spite of myself, feeling the inexplicable need to keep him talking. It was rare that I saw this side of him. A side unbound by the troubles that plagued us. A smile that was truly free.

"Same brother that kidnapped you from the stump?"

"Same brother." He nodded wearily. "He was two years older than me, stronger, and much better looking. Needless to say, I would *not* have introduced you. If he hadn't caught the fever, I'm sure the guards would have taken him instead..." He trailed into silence, looking abruptly lost.

It was quiet a moment, then I nudged him with a coaxing smile.

"He was one of three brothers?"

Will nodded swiftly, forcing himself forward. Perhaps it helped that he was standing right in the middle of his best childhood haunt. Memories were sweeter, the bitterness held at bay.

"One was younger, two were older. It was a crowded house," he added suddenly. "Crowded and loud. Everything was loud. I think sometimes I came out here just for the quiet."

I nodded warmly, trying to imagine it. "Five children...and you were right in the center?"

"A typical middle child," he answered with a grin. "Starved for attention, unappreciated savant, unquestionably superior in every way."

I snorted with laughter. "I think Claudie might have something to say about that."

He started to smile himself, but it faded almost immediately.

"She really hates me, Elise," he said quietly. "You should have seen her face..."

I slipped my hand into his, squeezing it firmly.

"You're doing this *for* Claudie. So that she can have a future. I *promise*, she'll realize that one day. And in the meantime, you're leaving her in good hands."

His face stilled a moment, then he nodded. "Miranda will take care of her. Even if I don't—" He caught himself quickly. "No matter what happens, Claudie will always have a place to stay."

He said each word quietly, as though reassuring himself more than me. His gratitude was overwhelming, but I could tell it appeased him somewhat to have given the woman something in return. Even if it wasn't the gift he'd originally intended.

As if thinking the same thing, his face brightened with a sudden smile.

"I can't believe you gave me that jewel."

I laughed shortly, having already forgotten.

"I can't believe you asked me for it," I teased. "What kind of a man takes a diamond *away* from the girl he claims to love? Maisy Dewhurst wouldn't have put up with such nonsense."

He laughed as well, raking back his hair. "It did seem rather backwards…"

We flashed each other a quick look, glancing away at the same time.

"Did you mean what you said?" I asked suddenly. "About moving somewhere else?"

A flutter of nerves churned away in my stomach, but I couldn't help asking him the question. Ever since he'd said the words, they'd been playing back in my mind.

Maybe somewhere by the sea…

A faint blush appeared in his cheeks, and while his eyes remained on the hills I felt sure his mind was elsewhere. A few seconds passed, then he answered with perfect nonchalance.

"Yes…if we can walk away from this. Claudie would love Nimoa." A few more seconds slipped past, then his eyes drifted slowly to mine. "It seemed like you loved it there, too."

My face flushed with warmth, but I lifted a shoulder with a shy smile.

"Why does that matter?"

The façade shattered for a moment and he glanced away with a grin. It looked as though he was prepared to give up right then, but as usual he took a slightly different approach.

"Because I'm going to need you to care for me when this is all over."

"Is that right?"

"I never learned to feed or clothe myself."

"Goodbye, Will."

A hand flashed out to my wrist, keeping me there beside him.

Looking back, it was a strange place to have such a conversation—perched upon a nostalgic stump in the middle of Reeves. But in a way, it wasn't unlike the other places where we'd had such moments. Tucked away in a plague town, hanging in punishment from the palace wall...

"Are you going to make me say it?" he asked quietly, turning to face me with a little twinkle in his eyes. "I have to take that risk by myself?"

I jutted out my chin, trying to balance on the cracked wood.

"I just got out of a rather volatile relationship. I may require a little coddling—"

The kiss came out of nowhere, stealing the words right out of my mouth. It weakened and dizzied me at the same time, buckling my knees as my arms wound automatically around his neck.

When he finally pulled back, he was smiling.

"Would you come to Nimoa with me?"

I bit my lip, staring up at him with a grin.

"Let me get back to you."

He pushed me off the stump.

Chapter 6

The next few weeks were some of the worst that we had. Not because of any particular hardship, though food was scarce and it rained for days. It was the uncertainty that was killing us.

By now, the blockade of the capital should have been in full effect. The crops that remained in Reeves should have been rerouted to other provinces and the ships of Nimoa should have shed their royal flags to work for the good of the realm instead. By now, our message should have spread from one corner of the map to another. Our small band of travelers had been commissioned to travel towards the coast, but the others had been tasked with spreading the rallying cry to Costan, Sackville, and the mines. The people should have united, the local troops should have been routed, and the beginnings of a grassroots army should have been well underway.

We hoped.

That was the problem. Travelling alone in the wilderness, there was absolutely no way to know such things for sure. And while we were confident in the resilience of our own people, there wasn't a doubt in our minds that those who had survived at the capital had not been idle in our absence, had been mobilizing as well. And much as we'd love a hopeful version of the story, there was an equal chance that things had played out rather differently instead.

Our friends could have been captured immediately; the three remaining provinces could have no idea the palace had even burned. When the troops had been driven back at Nimoa more soldiers could have been sent to overwhelm the dissenters, to reclaim the royal navy. Those trucks might never have come to Reeves. We might have been marching to our deaths.

Those were the kinds of things we *didn't* mention whilst hiking in the woods.

"I just love the rain." Zadie peered up at the violent clouds, squinting as a ton of cold water dumped upon her face. "The way it keeps you moving, keeps you clean. The way it *never* stops."

She fixed me with a watery glare, as though the further we got within my own province the more things like inclement weather could be seen as my fault. Demetrius flashed an apologetic grin behind her, wrapping a comforting arm around her waist.

"Would you like to ride on my shoulders?" he offered teasingly. "I'm sure Ella wouldn't mind traipsing through the mud, if you can get her to climb down."

It didn't matter what we went through—a shipwreck, a riot, a never-ending camping trip in the rain—the man was a rock. Perhaps it was merely the presence of his daughter, a tangible reason that made him incapable of breaking down. Perhaps it was a little something more.

"Don't be ridiculous," Zadie said stiffly, flashing the child a conspiratorial grin. "There's no reason why you can't carry us both. Isn't that right, Ella?"

The little girl smiled broadly, pulling on his dark strands of hair. "That's right. Don't be lazy, Daddy."

A chorus of tired laughter rose from the rest of us as we trudged over the rocky terrain. Thus far the journey had been relatively flat, with only the occasional ravine or dip of a river to interrupt the never-ending carpet of pine needles that cushioned our boots. Only in the last two days had the elevation steepened suddenly, bringing with it a new set of challenges.

The rocks were only the beginning. It was also getting harder to find food.

"Oh I'm sorry, princess. Are you having a hard time?" He rocked precariously, swaying her from side to side. "Perhaps we should switch places. You can carry me for a spell."

I chuckled at her raucous laughter before shooting a reflexive glance at Will. Of the entire group, he alone wasn't smiling. The very sight of the little girl seemed to cause him an unending amount of pain. I reached for his hand but he brushed it off quickly, flashing me a tight smile.

"Careful on the stone," he cautioned before I could say anything. "It's getting slippery."

There were plenty of things that could kill you in the mountains, but a simple fall could do the trick—especially in places where the foliage vanished to reveal the cracked granite below. Some of these cracks were shallow troughs, while others were deep chasms. Some of them merely caught your boot and caused you to tumble over the edge of the slope, crashing into the underlying forest.

It was the reason our progress had slowed to a crawl as we toiled onward, placing each step carefully as the face of the mountains grew slick with rain. It was the same reason that food had grown scarce, as most of the animals worth catching lived deeper in the trees.

"Are you sure this is the fastest way?" Isabelle asked quietly, picking her way across the stone beside us. "What would happen if we headed further south?"

"It's completely open and exposed," I answered briskly, shoving my hair back as streams of water trickled over my face. "We could try it, if you like. But if soldiers were to come..."

There was no need to finish the sentence.

The only chance we had against such forces was to stay somewhere they couldn't see, until such a time that our numbers overwhelmed their own. At this point, I could only hope the other groups were taking similar precautions as they trekked to the same place we were hiking ourselves.

And on that note...

"Why didn't you tell me about the station?" I asked Will suddenly. "You told the people in the other groups, those in Reeves; you even told Jasper, but you never mentioned it to me."

He flashed me a quick look, dripping little ribbons of rain. "Elise...do you remember much of that time?"

There was a hitch in my step—a flush of surprise, followed by the tiniest prickling of shame. The days following the explosion were still a blur to me. If it hadn't been for the people around me, there was no way I would have gotten from one day to the next.

"He told you a few times," Isabelle said kindly. "We all discussed it together—decided it was the only shared location that made sense."

The feeling of shame intensified. I had absolutely no recollection of such a thing. My eyes dropped to the ground as a familiar arm circled around my waist.

"Couldn't matter in the slightest," Will said dismissively, flashing a casual smile. "If anything, you missed some of Zadie's more memorable rants about the injustices of living in the wild..."

"Be careful."

I glanced up to where Demetrius was setting Ella cautiously on the ground in front of him, obviously judging it too great a risk of balance to continue with her on his back. Despite the slick stone the girl was absolutely delighted, straining against his protective hand.

"I'll be fine, Daddy! Let go!"

Isabelle and Will were still chattering away—determined to take my mind from the place it had strayed. She said something to make him laugh, but my eyes were still on the child.

"Absolutely not," he said sternly, tightening his grip. "You can walk on your own, Ella, but promise you'll stay right next to me the entire time."

Zadie closed in on the other side, blocking the dangerous slope.

"Your father's right," she said softly. "Listen to him."

"...convinced she'd seen a puma, but it turned out to be a raccoon. Sent me and Remy out searching by torchlight before finally admitting it might have been a dream..."

The wind swept down even harder, racing alongside the mountain's peak.

"Stop worrying," Ella whined, twisting away in the rain. "You never let me do—"

It happened so fast, I didn't even see her fall. One second, she was standing between them. The next, she had vanished into a crack in the mountain—leaving only the fading echo of a scream.

Time stopped.

"ELLA!"

Demetrius cried out in horror, still holding her cloak. The child had slipped straight out of the fabric, like something out of a dream. Zadie let out a gasp beside him, hands clasped over her mouth, while the rest of us froze in breathless silence, staring down into the abyss.

Only one person had the sense to move.

"Take this."

Without a moment's hesitation Remy handed off his things and slipped into the darkness, gone before any of the rest of us could register what he'd done. A ripple of shock swept over the mountain and we took a collective step closer, staring with aching anticipation into that endless dark.

The silence was impossible. In my mind, there were already two fresh graves. Then out of that endless nightmare, a familiar voice rang up through the stone.

"Will...I'm going to hand her up, all right?"

There was a crack in the stillness, a split second we dared to breathe. Then Will dropped immediately to his knees, reaching for the set of tiny hands that appeared quite suddenly, stretching out of the earth. He grabbed hold of them, pulling Ella to safety and passing her into her father's arms. Remy appeared a moment later, calm as ever, two sets of bloody scratches on his cheeks.

"Is she all right?" he panted, wiping off his hands.

None of us could answer. None of us had even moved.

There was a sound like a sob as Demetrius clasped the child to his chest, his entire body curved protectively around her, cursing himself for ever letting her go. Ella was crying. Wailing, in fact. Though she glanced back every few seconds to stare at Remy with wide, watery eyes.

"Tell me." he directed again, almost puzzled by our stricken faces. "Is she all right?"

The world commenced its turning. The people gathered lurched forward a step, then moved in earnest—surrounding the pair with a chorus of soothing voices, a mess of fussing hands.

But everything was *not* all right.

And it had very little to do with the child's fall into the mountain.

I stood alone at the edge of the crowd, staring with a peculiar expression at the steady tide of water streaming down from the mountain. While the others had almost tuned it out, bored and irritated with the constant challenge it presented, my own perspective abruptly changed—taking in the subtle changes that no one else seemed able to see.

The abrupt clouding of the water. The tangle of debris that swam in its wake.

"We need to keep moving," I murmured, though no one seemed to hear me. They were still gathered around Ella and Demetrius, almost delirious with relief. "We can't stay here."

Jane was backing away slowly, eyes widening as they drifted up the slope.

"Listen to me!" I shouted. "We need to leave!"

Slowly, excruciatingly slowly, the crowd fractured and turned my way. Will's dark eyes glowed like a light amidst the rest of them, cresting with confusion as they came to rest on mine.

"Elise, what are you—"

"NOW!"

As if to echo my shout there was a sudden noise from the peak above us, hard to identify, manifesting into a surge of pure dread. They needed no other catalyst. In a flash, we abandoned our plan to stick close to the valley floor and started scrambling to higher ground—grabbing on to each other with frantic shouts as we left that terrible rock face behind and raced into the alpine trees.

It was good they had listened.

No sooner had we reached a higher stretch of forest than a wave of frigid water thundered suddenly down the mountain—buckling our legs with its trembling weight. It surged past as we clung to each other in fright, strong enough to take down some of the younger trees beneath it.

A person wouldn't have stood a chance. I knew this firsthand.

"What the hell just happened?!" Zadie cried the second we could hear once again.

I stared down the mountain. The crack where Ella had fallen was completely submerged.

"Flash flood," I panted, still holding tight to Will's hand. "You can sometimes tell when they're coming. The water's darkness. It's filled with debris."

He trembled on the ledge beside me, unable to catch his breath. "How did you know that?"

I shared a quick look with Jane, followed by a little nod. "I grew up here."

IT WAS STILL MID-DAY when the water finally settled, but we made camp anyway—sticking close together until the sun had gone down behind the trees. Demetrius couldn't stop showering Remy with thanks, Ella couldn't stop crying, and Will couldn't let go of my hand.

He was still holding tight when we settled under our blanket, curled in each other's arms.

"I still can't believe that happened," he murmured, gazing up at the stars. The heavy rain had stopped not long after, leaving behind an ironic calm. "You saved our lives."

I shook my head silently, nestled beneath his arm. "Welcome to Sackville. Aren't you glad you wanted to come?"

He laughed humorlessly, gripping me tighter.

There were a few fires still crackling amongst the trees, sending up strange shadows as the flames danced and writhed towards the sky. I watched for a moment, then looked up at him.

"Why did you take me to that broken tree, back in Reeves?"

He glanced down with a hint of surprise, then rather deliberately looked away.

"I wanted to show you my places," he finally answered. "My memories, my haunts." He paused a moment before continuing, "I have very strong feelings for you, considering we don't know that much about each other."

I wanted to argue, but it was true. The bulk of what I knew about Will had come from eavesdropping when he was being interviewed by the scribe. Everything else had been gleaned in bits and pieces—short, truncated recollections whilst running for our lives.

I decided to argue anyway.

"That's not true. We...we know each other."

He smiled against my hair, eyes drifting once more to the stars. "Yes, we know each other. I feel like I know you better than anyone else...but those details are few and far between." He tensed slightly, then glanced down. "I didn't know about your father."

I stifled a sigh, staring at the fire.

"I don't like to speak of him," I deflected. "Neither did Remy, but you didn't press him."

"Of course not," Will replied. "That would have been wildly insensitive." There was a slight pause. "Besides, I already asked him back at the palace."

I laughed in spite of myself.

Of course you did.

"And?"

There was another pause, longer this time.

"A soldier raped his mother, that's all he knows."

The smile vanished from my face as my eyes shot automatically across the campsite. Remy was stretched out next to Isabelle, pretending to sleep—probably trying to avoid Demetrius and his continual stream of thanks. I stared in silence, watching the flames dance across his lovely face.

"Just someone passing through—"

"Someone stationed there," Will answered quietly. "They probably saw each other every day, but Remy never knew who he was—never had the heart to ask his mother."

I felt him glance down, his cheek resting on my hair.

"Is it something like that?"

The memories came before I could stop them, blurring my eyes and filling my head with a parade of foggy characters I'd rather forget. A group of people talking, tall men with cloaks and spears. My mother screaming at the window, a neighbor woman holding her back. And then a man with fair skin and dark hair like mine, flashing me a painful smile as he stepped out the door.

"My father is gone," I said shortly.

Will felt the tension in me and didn't press the matter further. It was awkward enough that he'd been forced to ask. Travel was virtually nonexistent in the provinces, and most everyone who ended up together had grown up just down the street, already knowing such stories themselves.

"...and your mother?"

He knew she was alive, I'd confessed as much back at the palace. But I'd come to realize that 'alive' was one of those relative terms. My mother's condition was a bit harder to understand.

"My mother...isn't right in the head."

He leaned back a few inches, lips parting in surprise.

"She isn't sick or anything," I clarified quickly. "She's just..." I trailed off, looking down at my hands. "When I was six, my father was caught stealing grain from a royal supply line. He wasn't a thief, but fever had just swept through the village and there just...wasn't any food. The troops decided to make an example of him. They gave him a choice: to die or enlist."

To most people it might have seemed an obvious decision, but the queen's soldiers were something worse than the devil himself. It was an unspeakable betrayal, what my father did.

"When they came to take him away, my mother just...shut down."

Will nodded slowly. This, at least, he could understand. He had seen such a thing many times in his own community. The moment of reckoning, when it all became too much.

"That must have been hard for you," he said softly. "To care for one such as that. When you were taken to the palace, did she—"

"I don't know," I interrupted. "I don't know what became of her. We always managed to make exactly what we'd need to buy food, washing the laundry of the village, but without me to drag up the water..." The cold truth settled upon me. "...I don't know if she'd even remember to eat."

Will looked at me for a long time.

"It shouldn't be this way," he finally murmured. "It shouldn't be this hard."

I sighed wistfully, gazing up at the stars.

"But it is."

It was quiet a moment, then his arms tightened.

"For now."

Chapter 7

The clouds were still gone the next morning, making the trauma of the previous day seem like nothing but a dream, as we spent the next nine hours hiking in rays of unfiltered sun. It was a welcome change of pace, but no one could quite shake the bitter adrenaline of the day before.

Case in point: my boyfriend wouldn't let me out of his sight.

"You're being *really* obvious, you know that?"

The two of us were walking in the woods, trying to find something the rest of them could eat for dinner. Rather, the three of us were walking. He'd brought along a friend to somehow mask the fact that he was incapable of letting me out of his sight.

"What are you talking about?" he scoffed, gesturing beside him. "*Remy* is here with us. How could you possibly think there's anything more to it than that?"

Remy rolled his eyes, trekking through the woods alongside us.

"*Remy* was taken against his will," he muttered. "*Remy* has been dragged along for ten miles just to prove a stupid point. Never mind that *Remy* was almost crushed to death in a storm—"

"That's right," Will asserted, clapping him on the back. "Look, you're upsetting him."

I pulled in a deep breath, glancing at the heavens for strength. "...this is just sad."

My newfound romantic imprisonment wasn't the only thing to have shifted since the flash flood. Temperatures had dropped sharply as well. Remy was used to such things—Bunkhill was quite close to Sackville in terms of climate—but Will couldn't stop shivering. He'd gone from the scorching plains of Reeves to the balmy weather of the palace, and had never known what it was like to be constantly cold. The chillier the woods became, the more his body subconsciously rebelled.

"How is this springtime?" he finally asked, glaring up at the sky.

The sun was nothing more than a mockery, light but no heat. Even that was fading as it dipped lower and lower behind the glistening trees.

Remy and I exchanged a quick grin before pushing onward.

"Too cold for your taste?" I asked innocently. "Maybe you could go back to camp, bundle up to protect that delicate temperament. Remy and I can handle this ourselves."

Will shot me a rather frightening look, while Remy sighed under his breath.

"Or maybe *Remy* could go back to camp," he murmured. "Get some rest—"

"I'm serious, this is ridiculous." Will ignored us completely, slicing through the dense underbrush. "You two can't possibly know, because you've been geographically brainwashed, but this isn't the way the world is supposed to feel in spring. I wouldn't be surprised if there was actual *frost* on the ground in the morning. I swear, this entire place is practically—"

He trailed off suddenly, staring through the trees with a look that chilled my blood.

Oh shit, what is it now?

My pulse started racing as I spun around to follow his gaze, reaching automatically for my knife. At this point, it could have been anything. Royal soldiers, bears, another flash flood—

"...what is *that*?"

The three of us froze.

Seriously?

It was a moose, as any child could see. A giant moose that was grazing in a distant clearing, the dwindling sun catching on its massive antlers as it lowered its nose to the grass.

I turned to Will in surprise, trying to determine if he was serious.

"Is that a joke—"

"Look at how big," Remy breathed in astonishment, frozen right alongside. "And those strange horns...have you ever seen such a thing?"

At this point, it felt very much as though I'd stepped into a parallel dimension—one in which my valued travelling companions had failed a basic vocabulary lesson and were staring slack-jawed across the grass. Twice, I opened my mouth to speak before simply rephrasing the question.

"Are you...*teasing*?"

Never had I felt the difference between our provinces so strongly. It was jarring and bizarre, yet strangely endearing. They stared in childish wonder, tilting their heads at the same time.

I suppressed a smile, staring at them fondly. "It's called a moose."

"Moose," they echoed in unison.

It reminded me of that first meal at the palace—where a sour-faced woman had taught Remy to say *caviar* for the first time. That being said, this creature was clearly a revelation; hunting was the last thing on their minds. I'd have to ease them into it slowly.

"You didn't have anything that big in Reeves?"

Will shook his head mutely, unable to tear his eyes away. "The occasional bobcat would wander down from the hills. Sometimes there were oxen...but those were tame."

Remy was staring in fascination.

"In Bunkhill we had snakes," he volunteered. "And bats."

Lovely.

I stepped in front of them, easing into their line of sight.

"We need to shoot it," I said gently, knowing that at any moment the creature might wander away. "We're lucky to have found it. We won't happen upon something so big again."

They nodded in unison, but didn't move a muscle. Remy was the one holding the bow, but it hung forgotten by his side. When creature tossed its head, they both lit up with matching smiles.

...they just named it.

I took the bow for myself, stealing an arrow at the same time. But no sooner had I lifted it to my chin than Will's hand flashed out and grabbed the string.

"Wait—" He caught my expression a second later and bowed his head, cheeks burning with shame. "Sorry, I mean...you're right. I'll do it."

With a final glance at the creature, he took the bow—but there was a wistfulness in the way he raised it to his shoulder. A second before he released the arrow, he actually shut his eyes.

WE ATE MOOSE THAT NIGHT.

The fellows were heartbroken, but tried to play it off. You wouldn't have known anything was wrong if Will hadn't been tracing his finger over the antlers, staring mournfully into the fire.

"Are you doing okay?" I asked him quietly, leaning against his side with a secret smile. "If you like, we can give that a proper burial just after dinner. You and me."

He nodded slowly, still staring at the jagged curves, then lifting it suddenly and jabbing it my direction. "So how do they kill people with these? Is it like *this*? Or more like—"

I wisely chose to sit elsewhere for dinner.

The meat had been a welcome surprise, lifting spirits after what felt like an impossibly long series of days. Stomachs were filled and conversation was plentiful, but not everyone had shaken the flood so easily. Jane was sitting a bit on the periphery as was her custom, shooting occasional glances towards the distant clouds, whilst Zadie appeared to have given up on life altogether.

Instead of occupying her usual position by the fire, the girl had slumped in comical defeat upon the leaves, limbs loose, crimson hair streaming like blood across the ground.

There was no one within several feet of her, as if they were worried her newfound angst might be catching. And when I perched carefully alongside her, she blinked up at me in a daze.

"You doing okay…?"

At this point, there was scarcely a need to ask the question. The girl had clearly shattered into a thousand little pieces—albeit, in her own perfectly Zadie-esque way.

"Oh sure…" She flipped a little on the ground, turning until she could dig her fingers into the wet earth, etching profanities and non-sensical pictures as mud crested around her nail. "I'm just waiting to see what's going to happen next. You see, I feel a little foolish. I thought nothing was going to top the palace. But then we set the palace on fire, blew up the train, got waylaid in a plague town, fled from soldiers in Nimoa, lost our ship in a storm, almost lost our lives in the heat that followed…and now we're sitting here. Having recently survived a flash flood."

I glanced bracingly at the fire, hedging my bets.

"Did you try some of the moose—"

"We're eating a moose."

She threw up her hands with a burst of laughter, showering those sitting too close in mud.

"That perfectly summarizes the experience." Her eyes swept over the crowd, landing on our two friends sitting in the middle. "You know, when you guys were dragging it back, Will and Remy looked about ready to cry?"

They'll be writing poetry about it before long.

"Honey?" I scooted closer, pursing my lips to keep a straight face. "Seriously, what's going on? Did something happen? Something I don't already know?"

Her eyes flickered in the distant fire as they stared into mine.

"You know the thing about an adventure?" she asked quietly, every hint of that signature humor fading from her face. "It brings out the best in people…for a short period of time. You get braver, stronger, calmer than you would have been before. You rise to meet the occasion, shocking yourself with the things you're able to survive. The things you're able to do." She paused a moment, considering. "But when it doesn't end…it starts to dissolve you."

My eyebrows shot up in surprise. "…*dissolve* you?"

She shifted restlessly, returning to the mud. "That's the scientific definition, yes."

By now, I knew better than to argue. I simply nodded along in agreement, pursing my lips with an amused smile. "And is that what's happening? Are you dissolving?"

She stared up at me slowly, hair strewn through the mud. "Me? I'm just fine."

Okay.

With a parting smile I patted her shoulder and pushed to my feet, leaving the fire behind as I rubbed some warmth into my arms and stared out over the mountains. We had climbed much further than intended to get away from the floods, but since waking up that morning we'd hiked almost all the way back down to the valley floor. We were close now. Very close to where we were supposed to be meeting the others. If I stretched on to my toes, squinting into the moonlit vista, I could almost see a glint of metal in the distance—the abandoned train station.

It didn't feel possible that I'd been there just a few months before. Herded into a panicked crowd with the others, absolutely terrified of what was to come. The longer I stayed in the woods, so close to my own childhood home, the more it felt like I'd never left.

Will had made so many passing references to Midlark, I had almost hit him in the face. But the longer I stood there, staring down into the valley, the more I wanted to turn around. To hike back up instead. Past the twin peaks that looked like the faces of bickering sisters, past the old cedar mill and the river where I used to haul of buckets of water for my mother.

For one of the first times since leaving, I allowed myself to think the unthinkable. To ask myself all those impossible questions I'd sworn never to ask myself again.

Did someone help her? Is my mother still alive?

"It's strange, isn't it?" I startled as Demetrius walked up beside me, seeing much further than I could with his arms folded across his chest. "Being so close to home."

I nodded silently, always forgetting that he and I were from the same place. The Durmont Crest he called home consisted of the entire range of mountains we'd been traversing. Somewhere, tucked away in those forested slopes, was the tiny village he'd called home.

"I didn't want to come back," I blurted suddenly. "Is that strange?"

I hadn't dared tell anyone. I hadn't even dared to say it out loud. Even now, standing in the dark, my cheeks burned with guilt and shame. But Demetrius only smiled, staring over the trees.

"Back at the palace...my chambers opened into a private garden. I would give my daughter baths in warm water. Every morning, we'd feast on candied fruit and champagne."

He turned that smile to me, if only for a wistful moment.

"It's hard not to think of those things, tainted as they are." His eyes flickered around the muddy banks and chilled stone. "It's hard to bring my child to such a place—a place so unlike any she's ever known. A place where children don't tend to last very long."

I nodded breathlessly, hanging on every word. There was a reason I'd grown so fond of the handsome man with the dark eyes. A quiet wisdom carried on that low, musical voice.

"Do you wish we had stayed?"

"No," he said decisively. "I never wish that. The day we left the palace was the day I started to live again. Only, sometimes..."

I leaned closer, staring up at him. "...yes?"

He flashed a parting smile. "Sometimes I miss the garden."

A distant face shot through my mind the second he walked away. Though we were standing on a crest of stone, I was overwhelmed with the scent of violets.

"But is that wrong?" I blurted again as he started to walk away. "To miss any part?"

He smiled again. A sad, sweet smile.

"A garden's just a garden."

THAT NIGHT WE KEPT the fire to a minimum. I didn't know how to explain it, just some collective instinct we all shared. Maybe the birds were too quiet. The second the last of the moose was smoked for the next day's hike, we brushed dirt over the flames and settled down to sleep.

Except that wasn't going to happen. Because there were more flames in the trees.

"Elise."

It seemed I'd only just closed my eyes when they shot open again—staring into a pair of faces hovering above me. Zadie was as manic as I'd ever seen, unable to keep from visibly trembling with excitement, while Jane was pale and grim—pointing up to the clouds.

"It's raining," she said without preamble.

I squinted upwards as a growing trickle of water streamed down onto my face. My hair was still half-dry, so it must have just started, but already the clouds were churning with a coming storm.

Again.

"She can see that it's raining," Zadie said impatiently, trying to shove the girl aside. "Elise, sit up for a moment. I need you to tell me what you see."

Remy and a few others were already gathered behind her. When I pushed onto my elbows in confusion, Will awoke as well—groaning wearily and leaning on his arm.

"What the hell's the matter?" he mumbled, sharpening slightly when he saw the crowd. "Tell me—what happened?"

"It's raining," Jane said more insistently.

Zadie looked ready to murder her.

"Sit up." She shoved both of us upward, then pointed over the trees. "What do you see?"

It took a moment to make sense of what she was asking. Another moment for my eyes to focus in the dark. But there was no denying it. A tiny golden flicker that could only be—

"Flames," I whispered.

Will sat up abruptly, cloak slipping from his arms.

"I can't believe it," he gasped, peering into the dark. Five or six distant fires glowed back at him, strong enough to have momentarily defeated the rain. "They got here so much faster than I—"

"Let's go!" Zadie cried, grabbing his arm and tugging him to his feet. "Who knows how long they've already been here! It wasn't until the sun went down that we could actually see the fires!"

I smiled along with the rest of them, groping blindly for my shoes. But amidst the flurry and excitement a pair of icy fingers wrapped around my arm. I glanced up with a start to see Jane kneeling on the ground in front of me. She alone wasn't celebrating with the others.

She looked worried instead. "Elise...the *rain*."

My eyes flashed around the campsite before returning to her face.

"What about it?" I asked with a hint of impatience. "So it's raining. *Again*. It's not that—"

"Yes—again." Her eyes burned into mine with unnerving intensity. "The sixth thunderstorm in three days. Such a thing is rare, even for these parts."

The others had gathered and were hiking gleefully downhill. I stood up to go with them but Jane shook her head, staying behind.

"We shouldn't go into the valley," she said softly. "Not until the storm clears."

"Elise—come on!"

I glanced down at Will, waving to me from further in the trees, before glancing back at the troubled girl still kneeling on my makeshift bed. My heart was pounding, but I tried to be rational.

"You're worried about another flood?"

She had begun muttering under her breath. "...loose soil, excessive run-off..."

"Jane," I said again sharply, "you're worried about a flood?" When she nodded slowly, I gestured to the distant fires. "If that's true, it's even more reason we need to reach the others. This storm just started. We'll help them gather their things, then take them to higher ground."

She stared nervously at the valley, chewing on her lower lip.

"Hey—we can't just leave them. They're not from this place, they're not going to move at the first sign of rain. They'll stay down there until morning. If it's actually a risk..."

I trailed off, letting her finish the thought for herself. But while she might have understood the logic behind such a reason, it wasn't enough to sway her decision.

"I'm staying here."

My mouth fell open and I leaned back in surprise. There hadn't been a single moment since leaving Nimoa that we'd intentionally separated from one another, no matter how dangerous things had become. Given that it was Jane, it seemed a particularly bad omen that she was abstaining now.

"Well...I can't," I said shortly. "Those are our friends down there. Someone has to let them know what's coming."

She nodded uneasily as I scampered after the rest of them, pushing to her feet and gazing up at the streams of water running down the slope. A little shiver swept over her, and before I left ear-shot I heard her voice calling out from amongst the trees.

"Elise—hurry!"

Chapter 8

With Jane's dire warning ringing in my ears I scrambled down the slope with the rest of them, slipping a little as the spongy ground beneath my boots loosened in the rain. Will caught my hand the second I was close enough, and together our entire group raced down the mountain.

We were fast, but quiet—moving with that same inexplicable caution that had made us limit our fires. It was impossible to tell which of our friends had reached the valley first—the group that had gone to Sackville, or Bunkhill, or one of the two that had been sent to Costan—but whoever they were, they were bound to be as cautious as we were. The last thing they needed was a group of screaming people bursting out of the trees. With our luck, we'd be shot on sight.

I can't believe this is happening, I thought euphorically, sprinting through the trees. *I can't believe they actually made it, that we're all circling back.*

After splitting off all those weeks ago, a part of me never expected to see them again. That part had intensified with each small tragedy that befell my own group. Surely, similar things had happened to the rest of them. Surely we weren't the only ones to have lost people along the way.

The rain stopped halfway down the slope, then started up again as we crept through the trees—first in a misting drizzle, then in heavier streams, so that by the time we got down to the valley, most of those fires had extinguished with a quiet hiss. We peered through the clouds of smoke that followed, heading swiftly towards them, trying to make anything out in the rain.

"It's them." Will quickened his pace. "I can't believe it's them."

His face shone with an emotion I hadn't seen in a long time, one he'd been too wary to let himself feel. As we got even closer, his fingers squeezed mine.

"This is going to work, Elise," he breathed, those dark eyes glowing like a beacon in the dark. There was a fleeting moment when they locked on to mine. "Everything is coming together."

One of the sailors from Nimoa pointed excitedly as he ran beside us.

"Look!" he cried. "They've even brought supplies!"

A chorus of delight rose up from the others as they pushed themselves even faster. I was right there alongside them, hurrying with all the rest. But in that same moment a familiar scent drifted through the trees, bitter and thick. I sucked in a breath and the smile froze on my face.

What is that? Where have I smelled that before?

No one else seemed to register the change. We were nearing the station now, quiet voices were filtering from the nearby camp. Zadie grabbed my arm, straining ahead with excitement.

"Can you see who it is?" she exclaimed, making no effort to lower her voice. "I thought Rachel's group was the closest, but if they stopped for—"

My hand flashed out in the darkness, clamping over her mouth.

Oil.

That's what I was smelling. The same kind of oil Eric had used to polish his armor. The same kind the capital used to supply its soldiers. I remembered the scent of it clinging to the commander's cloak.

There was a gust of wind, and it swept over the rest of them—freezing every single person in their tracks. We were close now, too close to turn back. Close enough to hear the jangling of armor, see the sharpened point of a spear. My blood ran cold as I stared in horror.

Our friends might still be coming. But they hadn't lit the fires.

"A CURSE ON THIS ENTIRE wretched province," a man's voice rang out in the sudden stillness, cold and sharp as a knife. "I say we take whatever explosives were left in the mines and blow these mountains straight off the map. We'd be doing the world a favor."

We crouched down at the precise moment the smoke cleared to reveal two people standing along the edge of the forest, poised between a large tent and the remains of a dying fire. There was something on the ground between them, but I couldn't tell what it was. As for the pair themselves, there was no mistaking them. Their faces were permanently burned into memory the first time I'd seen them at the palace. They'd haunted my dreams often enough in the nights since we'd left.

Count Lecron and the Countess of Baraque.

In the corner of my vision, I saw Remy freeze perfectly still then melt back into the foliage beside me. His face was so pale there was a chance his heart had actually stopped. There was a quiet gasp somewhere behind me, and I realized all at once what was on the ground between them. Not something, but someone. A heartbreakingly familiar face. Eyes open, staring lifelessly at the sky.

Joseph.

It was impossible to see what had killed him, only that there were flecks of blood on his face. Both hands were curled, but his arms were open—as if he'd fallen suddenly where he stood.

I covered my mouth with trembling fingers, unable to tear my eyes away. A trusted friend of Matthew's, the escaped servant had been leading one of the largest expeditions—almost thirty people.

Where are the rest?

"Not that I particularly care," Lecron continued speaking, unconcerned that he was standing just inches from the boy's curly dark hair. "I'd sooner cut off my own ear than return to this place."

The countess ignored him, staring at the body.

"Brave boy," she murmured.

Lecron glanced down in surprise, as if suddenly remembering it was there.

"You certainly played with him long enough," he chuckled under his breath, nudging the tattered jacket with his boot. "Feeling a bit frustrated, Margarette? This one had a lovely face, to be sure, but perhaps you were searching for someone else?"

I felt, rather than saw, Remy recoil beside me. Isabelle was just a few paces away, hiding in the shadows, frozen dead-still the moment she heard Lecron's voice.

"Given that we're in the middle of the wilderness with nothing but spears, I'd advise you to hold your tongue, Alexandre," she replied briskly. "Otherwise, you'll see how frustrated I have become. At any rate, the boy gave us nothing. It was a dead end."

Lecron shrugged, staring over the camp.

"We have the time," he murmured, lips curving in a little smile. "After what happened at the palace, we have all the time in the world..."

There was something strange about the way he said it, a superior slant to the words I didn't understand. The countess must have noticed it, too, because she looked up at him sharply.

"I was surprised about Hector," she said bluntly. "The man was standing right beside me in the chapel, closest to the tunnel, yet he perished in the fire like all the rest."

There was a moment of silence, a moment where Lecron's face reddened in the firelight and it looked like he was considering backing down. Then his glittering eyes shot up to meet hers.

"An unspeakable tragedy," he said with a catlike smile, "though you can rest assured the man was dead before he burned. I take comfort in the fact that all his gold flowed back into the royal treasury, to fund whatever expeditions the rest of us should desire."

My lips parted in astonishment, and Zadie jerked back like she'd been struck. I'd heard the two men bickering about such things before, at the picnic to celebrate my engagement. But never would I have imagined the wicked count might take matters into his own hands.

The countess looked at him in shock.

"Come now, Margarette—what was the point of it anymore?" he hissed. "The deed was done. I never understood why we were bound to stay together in the first place."

She looked as though she had some strong thoughts on the matter but she kept them to herself, turning back to the camp instead. It was far smaller than I would have expected, just a company of infantrymen. Still more than enough to destroy whoever might stand in their way.

"The others saw what happened to this one," she said quietly, eyes returning to the gasping flames. "We'll try one of them in the morning, though I expect we're in the right spot."

My heart sank like a stone.

Of course they had predicted such a thing—how could we have possibly hoped for anything different? What other meeting points could a group of far-flung strangers possibly have?

Lecron flashed a dark look, muttering under his breath. "The men of Nimoa didn't surrender so easily."

"They will be dealt with in time."

So the fires of rebellion were still burning in Nimoa. That alone was an unspeakable relief. But who were the others the countess spoke of? Were they already—

...that's when I saw the cage.

A silent gasp escaped my mouth as I stared through the splattering raindrops to the group of prisoners gathered on the other side of the encampment. It wasn't only Joseph's group—one of the bands that had travelled to Costan had been captured as well. They had already been beaten by the soldiers. Many times, by the looks of things. Those few who remained standing were huddled together in a silent cluster, staring through the bars with glazed, reddened eyes.

As I watched, one of the soldiers dragged his sword along the rusted metal. Laughing loudly when, at the last moment, it dipped playfully through the bars, slicing an unprotected arm. The boy inside gasped in pain, but did not cry out. Cruel punishments had been given for noise.

"Bunch of troublemakers," Lecron chuckled again, hand drifting to his own sword. "And those looks of shock when we came through the trees? What did they expect would happen?"

I waited for a callous reply, but Margarette shook her head.

"You blame them?" she asked softly, never taking her eyes off the bars. "You would blame a caged animal for trying to escape?" The count glanced at her in surprise but she continued speaking in a low murmur, eyes dancing with the dying flames. "Our greed knows no limits. Imagine if we'd left them alone. They'd still be tending the fields, mining the hills...instead of raising an army." She knelt down beside Joseph, touching the curve of his cheek. "Brave boy," she said again. "He never stood a chance."

A cold hand closed over my cloak, pulling me back into the dark. I turned the second I was out of sight, expecting to see Will. But it was Isabelle—trembling like mad and pale as the dead.

"We need to leave," she whispered, black strands of hair in her face. She spoke with a strange disconnect, as though a part of her was no longer there. "Elise, we need to hurry—"

Hurry.

The word echoed in my memory, like a leaf floating to the surface of a pond. In a flash of lightning, I saw Jane's silhouette watching from the top of the mountain. The rain continued to fall.

"We can't leave them," I murmured, gazing across the sea of tents at the cage. It was over a hundred yards away, but still, I imagined I could see every face. "We can't leave them here to die."

The sailor shook his head, backing into the trees. "We have no way to fight such numbers. We haven't even any blades."

"But we can't just leave," I insisted, straining towards them. "You heard what she said—" A hand was shaking me, another was holding me back. "We asked them to come—"

"*Sweetheart.*"

I blinked in a daze as Will appeared right in front of me, a look of quiet panic etched into every line of his face. To my shock the others were standing behind him, poised just a few steps from the trail we took down the mountain, ready to go back.

"What are you doing?" I asked in shock, pulling my arm slowly from his grasp. "Will, we cannot just *leave* those people here."

"And we cannot free them either," he replied roughly, as though it was causing him physical pain to speak. "Elise, he's right. We would only be captured ourselves. We haven't the numbers."

I cast a frantic look over his shoulder as the soldiers harassed them once again.

The names escaped me, but I knew the faces. The boy with the hurt arm was a captive from Reeves who'd been claimed by a duke. The pregnant girl with the flaxen hair was kneeling in the corner, one hand protectively over her swollen belly, staring without blinking into the rain.

"We haven't the numbers to fight...but we need only to unlock the cage." I grabbed the sleeve of the person standing closest, speaking without thought. "If we can just—"

"No," the sailor stated as he continued backing away. "No, they are already lost. I'm sorry for it, but there's nothing to be done. We need to regroup. Try to intercept the others before—"

That's when I started running.

I don't know what provoked it, or why any part of me thought it might actually work. If I'd paused for even a moment, I might have thought it was suicidal to take off sprinting through the center of an enemy camp. I might have found it foolish indeed that my eyes weren't on the idling soldiers. They weren't on the count and countess, or even on the cage of prisoners.

They were on the streams of water coming down from the mountain.

Dark as the storm clouds. Filled with debris.

I glanced back only once, long enough to see Will standing frozen in the center of the crowd, looking as though his very life was slipping away. Our eyes met for a fleeting moment as I pointed to the rain, then pointed to the peak. It was a silent warning, but the message was clear.

Get up the mountain.

"NO—"

He started to scream but the sailor struck him from behind, dragging him backwards as the others raced out of sight. A few more people tried to chase after me. Remy, Zadie, and even Isabelle were held back by people I would never see. My eyes were turned forward now as I left the safety of the woods behind me and flew without thinking, straight into the heart of the enemies' camp.

Time slowed to a ridiculous crawl, illuminating every petrifying moment.

For a few seconds, the soldiers were too stunned to stop me—freezing in various positions as my feet splashed through the rain. For a few seconds even those two plotting devils, the count and countess, stood perfectly motionless by the hissing fire. Mouths open. Speechless with shock.

It wasn't until I'd almost reached the other side of the camp that one of the guards saw fit to run after me. But by that time I had already picked up a sword.

I heaved it without thinking at the lock on the iron door—hitting it with such force that the blade vibrated right out of my hand. I was still reaching to retrieve it when the first of the guards caught up with me, kicking out violently as the countess screamed something across the camp.

His boot caught me in the ribcage, knocking the air straight out of my chest. A broken cry escaped my lips as my body flew backwards, rattling the bars of the cage. There was a wall of sound coming from behind me, a dozen shouting voices, but they all seemed to be saying the same thing.

"The sword! Give us the sword!"

It was the last thing I was able to do.

With a frantic hand I caught the weapon by the blade and shoved it backwards, watching in my periphery as a pale hand dragged it quickly through the bars. The noise intensified as a violent *clanging* echoed through the rain, timing out with surreal perfection to the advancing soldiers' steps.

Then a heavy fist connected with my face. I have trouble remembering after that.

An explosion of pain left me momentarily senseless, darkening my vision and crumpling my body to the ground. The picture throbbed in and out of focus. There was a splash of water, the warbling echo of distant screams. And something closer. A pair of boots—right in front of my face.

"That was very foolish, little princess."

Little princess.

That's what was looping through my head when he grabbed a fist of my hair, lifting me right off the ground. My eyes watered involuntarily as I dangled in front of him, so close I could see the manic gleam of adrenaline flashing in his eyes. The countess was still shouting somewhere behind him but he decided not to notice, smiling hungrily and taking out a knife with his free hand.

Another deafening *clang* echoed behind me. Followed by a muted *thud*.

From the corner of my eye, I saw the door to the cage swing open. A dozen blurry figures swarmed outside, clinging to each other for support. I wanted to cry out for help. I wanted to warn them what was coming, tell them to get higher up the slopes. But it was too late for that.

My eyes locked on the soldier, watching in slow motion as he lifted the blade. It glinted once in the moonlight, hovering for a small eternity above his head before streaking down—

"NO!"

Will came out of nowhere, leaping into the air with a feral scream.

There was a split second where both the soldier and I lifted our eyes in astonishment, unable to understand how he'd gotten there so fast, then a violent impact shattered the image as he tackled the soldier to the ground. The three of us tumbled onto the rain-soaked dirt, thrashing in a tangle of limbs before finally rolling to a stop. Will cracked his head upon impact, the soldier was lying face-down. Only I caught the glint of silver, shining just a few feet away in the mud.

I scrambled forward with a gasp, fingers closing around the handle, just as the guard roused himself and kicked me back to the ground. His lips stretched into a sneer when he saw the knife.

"Really?" he taunted breathlessly, casting a quick over his shoulder to make sure Will was still down. "Think you can manage it?"

No, probably not. I tossed it behind him instead.

The man was still turning in confusion when Remy caught the blade by the handle, twirling it once in his hand. Without a second's pause he plunged it twice into the man's neck, splashing blood each time. There was a strange gurgling sound, then the guard collapsed—sinking into the mud just as Will's eyes fluttered open and he pushed swiftly to his feet.

We stood there for only a moment, then we were in each other's arms.

"I'm sorry," he breathed, running his hand along the back of my head to check for any damage. "I got here as fast as I could—"

"There's no time," Remy interrupted quickly, grabbing us both by the cloaks and dragging us into the trees. "We have to go."

There were more people sprinting towards us, shadowy figures blurring in the rain. The ground itself seemed to be trembling as the storm

Jane feared so much picked up speed, rumbling down from the higher peaks across the wooded plain.

As for the prisoners? They were already heading up the mountain.

The soldiers racing through the encampment after them didn't understand it. We were effectively trapping ourselves. Why would we do such a thing? I cast a quick look around as Will pulled me forward—not understanding the scene myself. Why weren't they coming after us?

Only then did I realize my friends had a plan of their own.

Instead of simply racing into the clearing as I'd done, their approach had a bit more strategy involved. They didn't go for the prisoners. They went for the fires instead. Whatever scattered flames hadn't yet been doused by the storm were quickly extinguished—plunging the entire camp into a sudden impenetrable night. It was the only thing that had saved us. But it was only the first strike. While the soldiers rushed around, looking for torches and weapons, they unhitched the wagons carrying the royal food supply and sent them rolling down the valley slope.

Half the soldiers took off after them. A quarter of those who remained were still trying to light the torches so they could see. Meanwhile, those of us who'd grown up without such luxuries and had spent the last few months wandering the wilderness alone, streaked bravely into the forest, seizing every unchallenged moment to climb as high and as fast as we could.

There were just a few things working against us.

"They're not going to make it!" Remy panted.

Will and I threw a glance over our shoulders, following his gaze to where scores of injured prisoners were doing their best to claw their way through the trees. The rain wasn't helping. Neither was the water already streaming over the ground. Within a matter of seconds it had risen an extra six inches, pushing hard against every step they managed to take.

Several had already been struck down by the few soldiers who'd chased after us without the benefit of light. Those who remained were indeed struggling.

As I watched, one of the servant girls from Reeves lost her footing on the slippery incline and tumbling backwards towards the guards. There was a panicked shout as those who'd been running with her froze a split second with indecision, then continued racing up the slope.

The guards paused their pursuit as she fell, waiting with swords and smiles.

"Shit," Will cursed under his breath, then made a frantic grab for Remy's cloak as he turned around and sprinted back down the hill. "Remy, *no*! It's too far—"

CRASH!

A sound like an explosion shot through the forest and the ground shifted suddenly, throwing us off our feet. I landed hard on my stomach, gasping in terror as little tremors shivered down the mountain, vibrating through my palms. The first sound was just a warning. The second blew it away.

In a sudden rush, a literal wall of water swept through the forest—sweeping away trees and boulders in a churning, violent tide. The ground itself gave way beneath it, melting in submission as it carved a deadly groove straight down the side of the slope.

It passed beneath us. That was the only thing that saved our lives. Not until a moment later would I register that it had actually separated us from the soldiers. As it stood, all I could do was watch in frozen terror as it thundered straight towards the lovely servant girl from Reeves.

She never saw it coming. She was so intent on escape that she didn't know what was happening until the ground vanished beneath her feet. A piercing scream rang over the forest as she fell in what felt like slow motion, hands grasping desperately in front of her...

...only to catch hold of Remy's sleeve.

YES!

He'd lurched to a sudden stop, staring with wide eyes as the water surged towards him. But the second it passed him by he'd started running again, catching the girl just as she started to fall.

"Hold on!" he gasped, straining to pull her over the side. "I've got you!"

An arrow buried in the ground by his feet. By the time his head snapped up, two more had lodged in the dirt nearby. The soldiers might have found themselves temporarily stranded on the other side of the water, but didn't mean they didn't have other ways to fight.

"Remy!" I screamed, watching in a daze as two more people appeared beside the soldiers.

With a swipe of his arm, the taller of the two grabbed the nearest bow and nocked an arrow himself—firing it with deadly accuracy into the rain.

There was a spray of crimson as it buried in the girl's neck.

She must have died instantly, but it took a moment to register on Remy's face. He was still holding on to her, still bracing his entire body against the strength of the tide. When her fingers went loose on his arm, he pulled even harder—not realizing until a moment later there wasn't a point.

He scrambled back with a gasp as she slipped into the water—vanishing with a bizarrely peaceful expression beneath the rushing current. By the time he pushed to his feet Lecron had already lifted a second arrow, aiming over the water as a wicked smile danced across his face.

"Your little peacemaker," he muttered, fingers tightening on the shaft. "It seems you'll get the chance to watch him die after all."

Remy had frozen perfectly still. There wasn't any reason to run. The count's arrows were swift and true—they would hit their target whether he tried to escape them or not.

But he wasn't staring at Lecron. He was staring at the woman by Lecron's side.

Never in my life had I seen such a thing, the silent connection that held them. It was as if the last few months had never happened. As if the rest of the world had simply fallen away.

The count was still talking, the bow tightened in his grasp.

Only then did Remy seem to realize what was about to happen. His lips parted as some indecipherable expression washed across his face. Some part of it was an apology. Some part was pure defiance. More than anything he looked uncontrollably, overwhelmingly sad.

Margarette took a compulsive step forward as he pulled in a breath, blinking the rain from his eyes. His shoulders squared and his head shook with a little nod, waiting for the blow to come.

"Would you care to do the honors?" Lecron asked with a dark smile. "Or shall I?"

The countess looked at him, glanced back at Remy, and then she did something I'll never forget. Without a single hint of warning, she slid a dagger across Lecron's throat.

Even so far away, I saw how Remy paled in shock.

It was as though some invisible force had released him. His hand drifted to his chest and he took a step closer to the river, staring at the countess as the current rushed in between.

The storm thundered above them. Flashes of lightning ripped the sky.

Then, faster than my eyes could follow, a mighty wave raced down the mountain, even stronger than the one that came before. It swept across the ground where the countess was standing, taking her away as it tumbled down the side. Remy screamed in horror, reaching out his hand.

"Margarette!"

But she was already gone.

Chapter 9

The storm was over, but the damage remained.

Matched against an opponent neither could fight, the two sides—the soldiers and the captives—slipped away in defeat. With that violent slice of water still coursing between them, and with so many casualties on both sides, there was little other choice but to regroup.

They returned to the valley. We headed in silence up the mountain.

Jane was perched on the edge of the bluff by the time we finally made it back to camp; I hadn't imagined seeing her standing there in the storm. I flashed a weak smile as we shuffled past, half-imagining that I had, but it was easy to see she hadn't been idle in our absence.

Never one to partake in the logistics, the strange girl had made an uncharacteristic effort to prepare things by the time we got back. Two fires were roaring—an unlikely occurrence, given the constant drizzle of rain—and several buckets of water had already been collected and boiled.

I stared curiously, wondering why she'd felt the need. Then my eyes flickered to the newly freed prisoners and the obvious truth came to me.

We're not going anywhere. We're not in good shape.

I stood on the bluff with Will, watching as one by one the people who'd managed the climb dropped to the ground alongside the fires—making half-hearted attempts to warm themselves, to assess their injuries, and to avoid thinking about those friends who had fallen behind.

One of the men from Bunkhill took a single glance around, then set up a little station for himself beside the boiling water—gathering what supplies he could and waving people forward.

"He used to be a medic," Will murmured, staring at the painful procession. "Remy told me they used to bring him the people who'd fallen in the mines..."

Perhaps there was more to the story, but the moment he'd said the name both of us turned at the same time—watching as our gentle friend climbed slowly over the edge of the bluff.

It had taken some time for him to climb back up the mountain, drifting along the back of the group and keeping to himself. Truth be told, it had taken some time for him to leave the water.

The instant Margarette vanished beneath the waves, it was as though his feet had frozen to the ground. It didn't matter that soldiers had gone after the countess. It didn't matter that he was still within easy reach of their arrows, staring in horror at the exact spot she'd disappeared.

It wasn't until Will doubled back and grabbed him, literally dragging him up the slope, that he snapped back to the present, yanking himself free and continuing on by himself.

We hadn't known what to say to him then. We didn't know what to say now.

"Give him some time," I murmured, taking Will's sleeve when he tried to follow. "You would want some time...if it was you."

To be honest, I didn't think that was true.

Will hadn't thought twice before locking Lady Rosalynd inside the burning chapel. The woman had been a torment and nothing else. But the same couldn't be said for Remy and the countess. And that wasn't even taking into account the girl who'd fallen into the water.

Fortunately, Will didn't press.

He hesitated a moment longer, then nodded in silence—watching as the people who'd been trapped in the cage filed silently towards the healer. The pouring rain had washed away most of the blood, but there was clear damage in the way they were holding themselves.

There was clear damage in the way they were staring back towards the valley.

How long were they in that cage? I wondered, staring between them with tears in my eyes. *How many died before they could escape?*

As if hearing my thoughts, Zadie appeared beside us.

"Twenty-three," she panted, pausing to catch her breath. Since stepping out of the woods, the girl had been a constant flurry of motion. "That's how many survived the camp."

I turned to look at her slowly. "...how many started out?"

She hesitated a moment, then shook her head. "More than that."

Joseph.

Even now, having put some distance between myself and the valley, I still couldn't believe what had happened. I couldn't reconcile the image of him staring blankly towards the sky, while Lecron's boot rested absentmindedly beside his face. Matthew had known him, trusted him. He'd wanted to stay in the plague town—desperate to keep the people around him safe.

There wasn't even a body to bury. For all I knew, he'd been washed away in the flood.

"You were right."

I glanced up suddenly, to see Jane standing in front of me in the rain. She didn't flinch at the water the way most people did. Her eyes were clear and steady.

"You were right to go down the mountain, to warn them of the flood." She glanced a little sheepishly around the clearing, cataloguing all the new faces. "I forget those things sometimes."

Those things?

It was hard to know what she was talking about. The need for people? The need to save them? Sometimes I thought she would have preferred the company of that farm equipment instead.

My eyebrows rose, but I shook my head dismissively.

"That's all right. You told me the flood was coming." I followed her gaze, lingering on each new person who'd dragged themselves out of the storm. "That's the reason they made it out alive."

Will's eyes tightened and he bowed his head.

"I'm sorry," he murmured under his breath. "I'm sorry to have said—"

"You wanted to save me," I interrupted quietly, flashing a sad yet reassuring smile. "You wanted to save everyone who came with us. How could I possibly fault you for that?"

I meant the words with all my heart, but it was clear he was faulting himself.

Another wave of guilt crashed upon his face and he turned silently from the spectacle. It wasn't until a breathless cry rang through the clearing that he turned back in alarm.

"It's all right," the healer said breathlessly, holding the pregnant girl with the flaxen hair. His eyes flew up, searching automatically for Joseph before coming to rest on me. "There's been too much strain on her body, but I don't...I don't have the things I'd need..."

He trailed off, glancing around the muddy camp.

"She needs to *rest*."

It was never supposed to be a permanent settlement. And he was right, there weren't many supplies. For one of the first times, there wasn't even much shelter—we were standing in the rain.

The girl wailed behind him, eyes shut tight with pain, and I remembered Jane's ominous warning back by the lake. That the child would be premature. That the mother wouldn't survive.

My eyes flashed to hers for a brief moment before traveling slowly up the peak. "I know a place..."

I AM GOING HOME.

How many times had I dreamt the words? How many times had I stopped myself from saying them? Considering I'd only spent a few short weeks at the capital, my childhood village had washed away like something out of a dream. Lost in the certainty that I'd never go back, my mind had done everything it could to erase it. Blurring the edges and swallowing details, until my room at the palace seemed a lot more real than the place I'd been born and raised.

And yet, the closer we got the faster it returned to me. My pulse quickened and my eyes warmed as they jumped from thing to thing. A part of me wanted to revel in it, pointing out each sentimental haunt the way Will had done at his own home. But a far greater part was absolutely terrified. By the time we saw the morning smoke of the village, I could hardly even breathe.

"I can't believe this is happening," I whispered, freezing involuntarily as distant voices rang through the trees. "I can't believe we're actually here."

Will paused beside me, holding up a hand for the others to stop.

Since the time of the plague, the rumors about Midlark had grown so dark and hateful I wasn't surprised that some of the others were craning their necks for a better view. There were some who'd said our village had survived through witchcraft and sorcery. Others claimed we'd avoided the deadly sickness by sacrificing each family's firstborn child.

I truly didn't know what the others expected to see when they peered cautiously through the sunlit forest, but as my breath returned to me there was suddenly a single person on my mind.

...*Mother.*

In a flash, I was on the move—leaving the others behind even as they called out in surprise from the trees. The familiar scenery raced past, turning like the pages of a beloved book as I left the woods completely, bursting without a hint of warning right into the center of the village square.

Familiar faces glanced up in shock. There were shouts from ahead and more voices calling behind me. I heard the approach of fast-moving footsteps; no doubt Will was racing to my side. But I didn't pause for more than a moment before turning sharply and heading to the base of the village. To the little wood-cut house that stood by the edge of the forest. The one with the—

...with the lovely garden bursting into bloom?

I screeched to a halt, stopping so suddenly that Will crashed into me from behind. His hands came down on my shoulders—half to steady himself, half to keep me from running away again.

But I wasn't going anywhere. The second I saw the flowers, I'd frozen perfectly still.

"You need to stop doing that," he panted, still carrying the scars from my impromptu dash through the royal camp. "Where did you—"

"The flowers," I breathed, tilting my head in astonishment. "Why are they here?"

To his credit, he kept whatever censure he'd been preparing to himself and turned to follow my gaze. Our eyes lingered a few seconds on the delicate fairy-slippers and bright splashes of iris. Lilies and larkspur. There were even a few violets, swaying in a gentle breeze near the back.

"I don't understand," I finally murmured, staring as though in a dream. "None of this should be here. This was my garden, my treasure. When I was taken, I just assumed they'd all died..."

My eyes rose slowly as the door opened and a woman stepped onto the porch.

There was something familiar about her—the dress, the hands, the hair. But it was a smile I'd only ever seen in photographs and blurred childhood dreams. The eyes were the most telling.

There was life in those eyes.

"...Elise?"

My heart stopped the second she said my name.

"Oh, my darling," she gasped, clutching her chest. "You've come home!"

THERE WAS NO REACTION on my part. Nothing at all to register my mother had spoken. It was as if the very bones that held me together had turned to ice—so rigid and fragile, a single gust of wind could shatter them.

Will glanced swiftly between us. This was not the woman I'd described, the one who'd retreated into herself the day my father was taken away. The one who'd stopped speaking, stopped living. The one whose mind had become a hollow tomb, commemorating a future that never was.

"Elise?"

I startled when she spoke again, as though slapped across the face. I blinked several times in rapid succession, waiting for my vision to clear. Then I took a faltering step forward.

"...what happened to you?"

Looking back on it later, the irony was overwhelming.

There I was, fresh from the palace, having trekked from one side of the realm to another. In all likelihood, she had never left the front porch. And yet there had been a profound change.

Her cheeks flushed and she bowed her head, much the same way I did myself.

"After you left—" She caught herself, starting again. "After you were *taken*...I realized that I needed to...that I couldn't...that it was time to start doing things for myself."

I stared blankly across the clearing.

How great of you to realize that now.

"We're so pleased to see you're well." Will shot a quick look at me then strode gracefully towards the house, extending his hand with a tentative smile. "My name's Will. Your daughter and I met at the palace. She's told me..."

All about you?

"It's a pleasure to meet you," he finished quickly.

She blushed again, but stepped down those last few steps to shake his hand. Their eyes met briefly before hers traveled over his shoulder—coming to rest on my face.

"I don't understand," she said in a hush, as though we were standing in a chapel or beside a grave. "How can you be here? I didn't think I was ever going to..."

She trailed off once again, staring in astonishment as a flock of people ventured cautiously through the trees, coming to stand beside me. They were all young, with wide eyes and pale faces, staring with the bracing readiness of those always prepared to run. Another group was fast approaching from the village, stopping on the other side of the cabin with matching looks of surprise.

"Elise?"

It was the third time she'd said my name. This time, I was finally able to answer.

"Mother...these are my friends." I gestured blindly with a wide sweep of my hands. At no point did my eyes ever leave her face. "They need...we need a place to stay."

There was still blood on their clothing. Tattered pieces and broken leaves trailed behind them on the ground. There was nothing but absolute silence from the people of Midlark, staring with just as wary an appraisal as those from the other provinces had examined them.

For a terrifying moment, no one had the courage to say anything.

Then my mother squared her shoulders with a smile.

"Then Midlark welcomes you."

Chapter 10

It was a twist that no one saw coming. Even my wildest of dreams would have fallen short. In a flash my notorious childhood village, pariah to the rest of the realm, became something more.

Midlark became a sanctuary.

Once the decision was made, the people rose to embrace it—throwing open their doors and offering what few provisions they had for the communal use of all. It was a surge of generosity I had never experienced, one I thought had been stamped out through years of toiling away in the cold.

In the beginning, my new friends were afraid to trust it.

Each time something was offered, they would make it clear they had nothing to trade in return. They didn't understand the coaxing hands, the kind smiles from those same people they'd come to believe were nothing short of plague-resistant monsters. But the storm had been hard, the soldiers had been cruel, and they were in no position to refuse.

By the end of the first day, they were starting to settle into things. By the end of the first evening, they had given up old prejudices entirely and hailed the tiny village as a blessing from God.

I had learned the hard way to be wary of blessings.

We had effectively killed the count and countess—so where were the reprisals? We had left behind at least half a company of soldiers—so why weren't they charging up the slope?

The floodplain was still there, cutting like a seam between us, but these men were heavily equipped. It would be hard to find the village, tucked away in such a large range of mountains. Hard, but not impossible. They had experience with such things. They could follow our tracks.

At least once a minute, I found myself glancing back towards the trees—still nodding or smiling along with the latest conversation. Still bracing for the sting of those swords.

About halfway through the afternoon, Zadie told me I had trust issues.

Will had nudged her into silence, then asked quietly if I'd spoken with my mother.

I'd abandoned both of them by the fire, wandering the village by myself.

In the months since I'd gone, nothing had really changed. The well was still broken. The spindly fence that ran around the forest was still in need of fixing. A series of rundown houses still framed the village square. The winter frost had broken, giving way to the cool sunlight of spring, but the roofs were still sagging from months of carrying the heavy snow.

I paused a moment, watching as one of the boys from Nimoa climbed atop a nearby cabin, helping the woman who lived there pull away the rotted boards to replace them with something new. He was still bearing the marks from the soldiers, but that sense of gratitude was overwhelming.

All because the mountain people had opened their doors.

All because my mother had asked them to.

My brow tightened as I continued my pacing anew. Much as I hated to admit it, Will's soft question had cut to the core. I was avoiding the woman. I'd avoided her every attempt to approach me since the fateful moment she'd invited us all to stay.

It wasn't fair. I was clear-headed enough to acknowledge this. Most people who had broken as badly as my mother never found a way to make themselves whole. I should be feeling grateful. She had welcomed us with open arms—I should be feeling grateful for that as well.

But I didn't. I felt angry instead.

There was a small commotion across the square as a pair of middle-aged people emerged suddenly from a cottage, leading a young girl between them, laughing nervously at some forced joke.

Jane.

If there was one person who was having a more difficult time with reentry than me, it was the pint-sized genius who'd warned us about the flood. She had gone immediately to the home of her parents, probably expecting to find that at least one of them had died, only to be greeted by a chorus of astonished exclamations and suffocating embraces. Their little girl had come home!

...and hadn't said more than ten words.

I supposed I should have been grateful for that as well, grateful I wasn't alone in it, but I only felt sorry for her. Even now, as they were showing off some inconsequential addition to a shed in their garden, she was staring straight ahead with vacant eyes—cringing under the hands of her mother, looking as though she wished we'd stayed down on the valley floor after all.

"She was very young when she left," a soft voice said behind me.

I jumped in spite of myself, glancing quickly as my mother came to stand at my side. She made no further attempts at contact, just stood there gazing in the same direction.

For a conflicted moment, that inner voice rang inside my head.

Embrace her. She's your mother. Be glad she can talk...and embrace her.

"When she was *taken*," I corrected, remembering how my mother had done the same. In an instant I turned to face her, staring right into those pale grey eyes. "You understand the difference?"

She flushed, but held my gaze—staring back with an expression I hadn't seen in a great many years. There was depth to it. There was gravity. It only fueled my rage.

After a suspended moment, she pulled in the breath to speak.

"It must have been very lonely."

My eyes flashed and I looked back to Jane. They were inside the shed now, gesticulating so wildly I could see them from the muddy street. "I made friends."

She glanced at me in surprise, then nodded to herself. "You certainly did." The most unlikely of smiles tugged at the corner of her mouth. "He is very handsome—the man you came with. Perhaps the most handsome man I've ever seen."

It should have softened me. I was clear-headed enough to see that as well. In a perfect world, I would have smiled. We would have shared a quick laugh before I rolled my eyes in adolescent rebellion and vowed never to bring him home again.

But our world was far from perfect. And you could hardly call this my home.

"Well, that's what the palace looked for," I said briskly, my eyes on the shed. "The court had exacting standards. Only the most appealing and attractive would be brought to their beds."

From the corner of my eye, I saw her flinch. It was a physical thing. As if someone had pricked her from behind. After a moment, her shoulders lowered with a silent breath.

"You were truly chosen by the prince of the realm?" she asked quietly. "You were truly offered a place in the royal family and walked away? Burned it all down?"

She hadn't gotten the story from me. One of the others must have told her while I was wandering about with a distracted frown. Instead of offering more words myself, I simply nodded.

She considered this another moment then glanced skyward, as though finishing some silent prayer. When her eyes returned to the shed, they were twinkling with a light and warmth I had thought was lost sometime in my childhood. I wanted to leave. But I couldn't tear my eyes away.

"Why are you smiling?" I finally demanded.

She glanced at me almost nervously, but couldn't hide that tearful happiness that had settled upon her face. "My daughter came home. I never expected to see her again."

I stared a moment longer, cold and remote. "I never expected to see my mother again, either."

There it was—that radiant smile of hers finally vanished. If I thought that would make me feel better, I was mistaken. Nothing made it better. Everything made it worse.

As if on cue, Will's gentle reminder echoed softly in my ear.

She is your mother, and she came back to you. At least you still have one. At least she's not lying in a grave.

Some light emotional blackmail, but it was hard not to see his point. Even if she hadn't found the strength to return, could I have really held it against her? What if I'd found myself in the same position? Freezing and hungry, clutching a child while armed soldiers took my husband away.

I would not have done as she did.

That little voice was back. This time, it was on my side.

I decided to ignore it, offering an olive branch instead.

"I'm sorry." I bowed my head with a quiet sigh. "You didn't..." *Deserve that?* "Since we've arrived, you've been nothing but generous. It's wrong of me to bring up troubles from the past."

She froze perfectly still in my periphery, then stepped directly into my line of sight.

"It was *wrong* of you?" she echoed incredulously. "Since the moment you set foot in the capital, do you honestly think you've done anything *wrong*?"

When I didn't answer, she shook her head.

"Elise...you were born in this wretched place, you grew up with an absent father, and the one person who was supposed to look after you turned into a premature ghost. When given the chance to correct all that, for the small price of your soul, you burned it down and walked away."

Each word was quick and sharp, shocking me to the core. How long had I wanted to hear her say them? How was it possible I'd never thought of what I'd say in reply?

"And I wasn't talking about the palace," she continued abruptly, those pale eyes fixing upon my face. "I was talking about Midlark. How lonely your life must have been, after...it happened."

It happened.

The closest we'd ever come to acknowledging it. For months afterwards, I was told by well-meaning neighbors and shrill, rasping friends not to mention the departure of my father anytime my mother was within vicinity of the house. It would only upset her, they'd said. It would only make it worse. Such threats were enough for a frightened child. Already a little too cold, a little too hungry, a little too sad for her own good. I mourned for my father in silence. Waited for him by the door.

It happened.

"You were in shock," I mumbled half-heartedly. "You were hardly the first—"

"It is unforgivable, she replied, blunt and crisp. "You should not forgive it."

There was a pause. There was always a pause with my mother, but those silences had never led to anything else. This one did. Those eyes found me once again.

"But I'm asking you to give me a chance."

The look on my face must have been incredible, because as soon as she said the words she hastened to temper them. To turn them into something we could both understand.

"Not to make things right," she said quickly. "That is a privilege I lost long ago. But perhaps to make things better. Easier. The chance to help you in any way that I can."

The silence was mine now, as if it had jumped from one woman to another. I didn't know how to break it. I didn't know what I must now be expected to say. Where were those neighbors and rasping friends with their shushing hands and their scripts? I was lost without them.

In the end, I was left with only the truth.

"...this helps."

My eyes strayed away from her to the rest of them.

Those who were able to walk had spent the hours milling aimlessly around the village. Those who weren't had gathered around the healer, perched on the edge of the little square.

Progress was being made. Wounds were stitching back together.

"Then this is what I shall do," she said with determination. Our eyes met ever so briefly before she headed back to the house. "In the meantime, I'll try to keep my smiles to myself."

Chapter 11

I was in the garden when Will found me, tending to the roses.

Not my garden, of course. Not my roses.

But I'd been there many times before.

"I've been looking for you," he called quietly, walking up through the grass. There was a house in the near distance, and he looked hesitant to trespass. "Zadie said you were—"

"I couldn't stand it anymore," I answered, still looking at the blooms. They had grown rather wild in my absence. The deliberate trails I'd cut between each plant had been overgrown with moss.

He didn't need to ask what I meant—we'd spent the entire rest of the night listening to the pregnant girl's screams. It was a kind of labor, that's what the healer had told us. A false trigger, the body's way of warning a mother to slow down. It was supposed to stop eventually. When she was still crying out in the morning, I'd wandered to the other side of the glen.

"This place is beautiful," he said softly, coming to stand behind me. "Do you know the person who—"

"This is the place I was taken."

He stopped cold, staring at the back of my head.

In hindsight, I wasn't sure exactly why I'd told him. I wasn't even sure why I'd come. Back in Reeves he'd taken me to the place that was the most important, that held his sweetest memories.

I'd gone to a garden where I'd been threatened by a man with a club.

"Well, that's..." He trailed off helplessly, searching for something to say. If I'd been in a better frame of mind, I might have felt sorry for him. After a few seconds, failing to find a way to temper such memories, he decided to shift focus instead. "...a lovely place to do it."

I looked up in surprise, but he was already drifting through the flowers.

"Did you come here much before?" His eyes swept up and down the little rows, once so painstakingly tended. "A lot of love has gone into this place."

I warmed in spite of myself, trailing after him like a shadow. "I came every chance I could. My mother had an arrangement with the woman who owns the property..."

My voice trailed off and my eyes flashed to the window.

The house was deserted, but I could still see her standing behind the curtains. Pretending not to watch as I screamed for help and the soldiers dragged me away.

Not so difficult to imagine, really. Not a thing had changed. Same curtains.

Will studied me a moment then continued that casual pacing, leading me further and further into the garden and away from the rest. Every so often he'd pause to examine something, tilting his head as his eyes traced over an unfamiliar array of petals or cluster of leaves.

It was the moose all over again, miniaturized and scented. He was right. The two of us had grown up in different worlds. There was still much to learn, many things we didn't yet know.

"The garden by the side of your house," he began thoughtfully, "your mother has been tending it?" His eyes shot ever so briefly to my face. "She's different than I thought."

I tensed involuntarily, then reminded myself to breathe.

"She apologized," I said almost brusquely. It was hard to be brusque in a garden. "She said that it must have been lonely all those years, when she'd...been away."

It happened.

I realized in that very moment that it was the only thing I'd ever wanted to hear her say.

"She said you were very handsome," I added suddenly, changing the subject. "Quite possibly the most handsome man she'd ever seen."

"Oh yes?" He glanced at me speculatively. "And your father is gone for good? I'm not stepping on a prior claim—"

I pounded two fists into his chest, erupting with laughter. "How could you *possibly* say that?"

He shielded himself with a grin. "Just keeping my options open."

"How could you possibly say the word *claim*?" I threw out my hands to the garden, then dropped them back to my sides with a breathless smile. "Here, of all places..."

He stood there grinning, as brazenly unapologetic as he'd been in the palace. Then, without a bit of warning, he swept forward and kissed me lightly on the cheek.

Our eyes met for a moment, then we continued walking.

"What's this?" he asked suddenly, kneeling down to examine a burst of flowers.

I knelt beside him, looking over his shoulder.

"It's called lissium," I answered. "It's all over these mountains, a native species. She probably didn't plant it. It grows where it likes."

There was some in my own garden. Others rooted it out when they could, but I was oddly taken with it. Such a striking shade of red.

I touched the petals, then glanced up with a frown.

"I told you this already—"

The words caught in my throat.

I didn't tell Will.

I told Eric.

He stared at me blankly, then shook his head.

"Sorry, I must have forgotten. At any rate, we should head back to the others." He pushed lightly to his feet, offering down a hand. "Those soldiers are still waiting at the base of the mountain, and as soon as the water subsides...we're going to need a plan."

I nodded hastily and stood beside him.

No point in dwelling on the past. Not when the future was barreling towards us.

BY THE TIME WE GOT back to the village, there was a strange tension in the air. A charged stillness that held the streets in an invisible grasp. It took me a moment to realize what it was.

"It's so quiet," I whispered, taking hold of Will's arm. "Why is it..."

The healer walked towards us, his tunic covered in blood.

"I couldn't save her," he panted, shaking his head. "I tried."

Why he felt the need to tell us, I would never know. Perhaps because we were simply walking towards him. Perhaps he would have said it regardless, whether we were there or not.

I took one look at his face, then my eyes drifted higher to one of the cottages across the street from my own. The door was thrown open, and through it I could see a cluster of people and tangle of bloody sheets. Isabelle walked out a moment later, carrying something in her arms.

"It's a girl," she murmured, cradling it gently. "She had a little girl."

My lips fell open, but no words came out.

The pregnant captive had died, just as Jane predicted. I didn't even know her name.

"She..." Will's voice trailed off as he stared once more at the cabin. "I thought it wasn't time yet. I thought it was supposed to subside..."

There were sounds now, coming from inside. People going about the grim business of clearing away the evidence of such a thing. Just another quiet tragedy, unmarked amidst all the rest.

"Should we do something?" he asked uncertainly, glancing between Isabelle and me. "Is there someone who needs to...? What should we do?"

I was at a loss, but Isabelle was transfixed by the bundle wriggling around in her arms. Even as we stood there watching a tiny hand reached up, wrapping around her finger.

"I can look after her," she murmured, almost to herself. There was a soft gurgling and her face warmed with an expression I'd never seen. "We can look after each other."

I had no idea what to make of this. My head was spinning and my legs felt weak.

"I tried..." The healer was still standing there, staring down at his hands. The rest of the world had kept turning but he was still back in that cabin, watching it play out again and again. "I'm so sorry, I..." He trailed away, shivering. "I didn't know what else to do."

A gentle hand squeezed my elbow.

"Elise," Will prompted softly.

The healer was speaking to me. Isabelle was speaking to me.

Any moment, those people in the cottage were going to empty onto the streets—their hands stained with blood, their eyes full of questions. Full of expectation.

A baby was crying for her mother...and people would be looking to me.

I should have stayed in the garden.

"Elise?"

I turned abruptly on my heel and headed towards the trees. Fleeing with no thought as to my destination. Fleeing only to escape. There was movement behind me, but no one followed.

"I'll...I'll be right back," I stammered, tripping over the foliage. "I just need to..."

The village disappeared, swallowed by the canopy of trees.

THE SECOND I WAS OUT of sight, I broke into a run—hitching up my cloak and going as fast and as far as my legs could take me. It wasn't wise to do, certainly. The only reason we'd returned to the village was to discuss the bloodthirsty army prowling just down the slopes.

But wisdom had abandoned me. There was no longer room for it in my head. Not with all those other things battling each other for prominence. Faces and stories, and those haunting cries.

I can look after her. We can look after each other.

My stomach heaved and I threw up, gripping on to a tree for balance.

In a bizarre way, it seemed the most impossible thing of all. They would look after each other? How would such a thing be possible? Where would they even go? We had been outed, treed like helpless animals. A newborn baby, but those troops would come for it all the same.

Why did I think this would work? Why did I bring them here?

The world spun dizzily and I stepped to the other side of the tree—sliding down to the very base as fresh tears ran down my cheeks. We didn't talk about such things to stay light, we didn't think about such things to stay sane. But the problem with such excellent compartmentalization was that every now and again you ended up in a wandering in a garden, having lost all sense of reality.

It didn't matter that I'd come back to Midlark. It didn't matter that my mother had returned from a realm of ghosts. It didn't even matter that the poor baby's mother had died.

We were *all* going to die.

They had an army. We were trapped in a village. Whatever people might have been coming to our aid would run into those swords first. There was nothing we could do to stop it. And now—

"—heard someone running through the trees."

My breathing hitched and the tears stopped cold. Like a puppet on a string I pulled myself to my feet in a single, lifeless motion, peering desperately around the tree.

...only to find a host of people staring back at me.

Those soldiers weren't gathered at the base of the mountain, biding their time.

That time was upon us. They had come for us now.

Get back to the others. Do not die out here alone.

"RUN!"

I screeched at the top of my lungs, sprinting straight back the way I'd come, without a prayer of getting there in time. Branches sliced my skin, and little bits of debris caught in my hair. My feet flew impossibly faster when I heard the sound of boots behind me, and still I continued to scream.

"TAKE COVER!"

I stumbled, my boots catching on a log.

"GET INTO THE—"

My voice cut off in a scream as I was lifted straight off my feet—whirling around to find myself trapped in the arms of a royal soldier. The tips of his ears had been burnt by the sun but his skin was shock-pale as he tried to control my flailing limbs, yelling something at the same time.

What he was saying, I'd never know. My entire world had narrowed to this one clarifying moment. The moment when my part of the story would be finished, ended by a stranger's hand.

He reached behind him and I braced for the blade—wondering suddenly if it would be quick, like I'd imagined. Wondering if he recognized me and would draw things out instead.

All the while he continued speaking, but I closed my eyes rather than look at him, trying to picture a different face. It wasn't the first time I'd done such a thing. Will's twinkling smile came easily to mind. I tried my best to hold on to it. Memorizing the details. Trying to smile in return—

"Cricket?"

It was perhaps the only thing that could break through—this one puzzling word that didn't fit at all with the others. My eyes cracked open, only to find that the soldier hadn't been reaching for a blade after all. He'd been unbuckling the strap on his helmet, pulling it off his dark hair.

There was a split second when my senses came back to me.

This wasn't a stranger. I knew that face. I knew those eyes. A shadowy recognition hung right on the periphery of my mind, sharpening into sudden focus when those lips curved in a smile.

"I wasn't sure if you'd recognize me. You were so little when I left."

I blinked once in astonishment.

Then I pulled back my fist and punched my father in the face.

Chapter 12

The official story was that I tripped on a tree branch. But the truth was, I blacked out.

I was told all of this later. I was offended, only later, that my friends had accepted the tree branch story without a second thought. At the time I knew nothing but my own dizziness as I sat up slowly on the cot where someone had laid me, lifting an uncertain hand to my head.

My knuckles were bruised. When did that happen?

There was a noise at the door. With a start, I realized that I was in one of the cottages along the village square. Not my mother's cottage—strange. Though, to be fair, I had gone out of my way to avoid the place since we'd arrived in my hometown.

"Elise?"

I lifted my head in relief as Will stepped inside. As usual, he looked just at home in a random village hut as he had back at the palace—moving with the same self-assuredness and casual grace.

His eyes told another story.

"Hey...how are you feeling?"

My lips parted, but I couldn't find the words. Quite possibly because I couldn't remember the story. We'd been in the garden, hadn't we? And then the healer...the baby...

I sucked in a quick breath. "There are soldiers in the woods."

They'd captured me. I'd run straight into them. How was it possible the two of us were speaking so freely? There had been over a dozen. Surely they'd overwhelmed our tiny group.

He tensed ever so slightly, but sank onto the bed beside me—taking my hand in his own.

"There were some," he admitted softly, "but it's not what you think. They left the company that had traveled with the count and countess.

Most of them are village people. After the flood, when their numbers were decimated, they saw a chance to return."

He paused ever so slightly.

"They brought you here. Carried you back."

I blinked slowly, trying to keep pace. There seemed to be huge gaps in the story, but it was too difficult to follow along. I felt as though I'd been dropped off the mountain. My head was spinning and it was impossible to ignore the searing jolts of pain in my hand.

"Something happened," I mumbled, staring down at the bruised joints. "Maybe I clipped it on something in the garden—"

"Honey?"

There was more movement on the other side of the door. Will cast a swift glance over his shoulder before turning back to me with a trace of panic.

"What do you remember from the woods?"

The woods?

I tried to sit up before sinking right back onto the cot. I didn't remember anything about the woods. Hadn't we returned to the village square? Isabelle had been holding a baby. Except that I *had* been in the woods. That's where I'd seen the soldiers. That's where I'd seen—

My face grew suddenly cold.

"...Elise?"

Both of us turned at once as the door creaked open and a tall man stepped inside. He paused immediately upon entering, hovering uncertainly in the frame. If I'd been in a different state of mind, it might have been an almost comical sight. The house was too small to accommodate such height. The tips of his raven hair brushed the weathered rafters. His eyes flicked up reflexively, as if he'd expected as much. As if he'd found himself in a similar situation before.

A second later, I realized that was precisely the case.

He'd helped construct the roof.

"I wasn't sure if you were awake," he began, looking uncertain as to where he should put his hands. They clasped first in front of him before winding around back. "They told me—"

"This is why I was brought here," I interrupted with sudden understanding, speaking only to Will. "My mother...she didn't want him in the house."

As if on cue, the door opened and the woman in question stepped inside. She took one look at my father, eyes screaming all those things she couldn't say. Then turned her back and swept across the room in five quick strides, kneeling beside the bed.

"How are you feeling?" she asked, sweeping the hair off my forehead.

It was a reflexive gesture, but I stilled in wonder at the touch. How long since she'd done something like that? How long since the three of us had been in the same room?

Why does ANY of that matter?

"Why are you here?" I asked sharply, levelling my gaze upon the man.

The man. It would not do to call him my father.

His eyes flashed swiftly between us and blinked quickly, as if he'd been asking himself the same nostalgic questions. Then he took a step forward before falling immediately back.

"I had hoped...I had hoped your friend would tell you." He shot a quick look at Will's and my entwined hands. "There are many in the guards who dream of a previous life, many who wish to return home to their families." His voice tightened at the word. "I didn't see you the night of the flood. If I had...things might have been different. But when I heard of it later, I rallied what men I knew shared the same sentiments and led them to the village. The bridges had washed out and the trails had worn away. It took some time...otherwise we might have gotten here sooner."

A ringing silence echoed between the four walls of the house.

This cannot be real. This has to be a trick of some kind.

"All this time, you've been at the palace?" Will asked uncertainly. I gave his hand a secret squeeze, grateful he could speak when my mother and I could not. "I didn't see you..."

It was a leading question and not entirely fair. The queen's army was vast and spread over the entire kingdom. Most had never been to the capital. Yet my father nodded his head.

"Not at the palace itself, but in the capital. Many battalions were permanently stationed to defend the perimeter—not that there was ever a need..." He trailed off again, the inner workings of the royal army the last thing on his mind. Those bright eyes traveled once more between his wife and estranged daughter before settling on the floor in between. "I have missed you."

My mother and I were statues. Will looked like he was praying desperately to be swallowed up by the floor.

"When I left the village...I'd always hoped one day to return." He paused ever so briefly, as if worried we might not believe that was true. "Men tried to escape on occasion, they were always brought back in chains. There came a point when I almost...I almost lost hope."

His eyes shone as they rested on my face. "You've grown up, cricket."

...and THAT'S my cue to leave.

STRANGELY ENOUGH, I didn't need to throw another punch or bolt from the cottage. I didn't even need to faint. The second he resurrected the old nickname, my mother sprang to life and escorted him firmly back outside. By the time Will and I ventured out ourselves, they were nowhere in sight. At this point, I could only assume she'd drowned him in the river.

An awkward silence fell between us, one made all the worse by the shrill voice that started yelling somewhere inside my house. After a few seconds, he cast me a sideways glance.

"So...cricket, huh?"

My eyes flew skyward and I sucked in a breath of cold air. It was easier to talk about such things out in the open, but the word still dug in like a thorn.

"It was his name for me," I replied. "I'd all but forgotten it until now."

Not true. I simply never allowed myself to think on it.

Will nodded casually, examining me from the corner of his eye. He waited a few seconds longer, then ventured a tentative, "You didn't *eat* one, did you?"

There was a beat of silence.

"William—"

"The same way you wished to be a pony?"

I prayed for strength.

"It was my voice, you insensitive worm. I had this little, chirping voice." My eyes lifted suddenly, staring towards my childhood home. "He used to read me these stories. There was a little stack of books by the fire, and every night he'd read me a different one."

It was another memory I refused to entertain, one so painful the thought of it brought tears to my eyes. Another lifetime ago, but I could still hear that rich baritone lulling me to sleep.

"When he left...my mother buried the books. She didn't burn them or toss them in the river. She didn't lock them in a cupboard some- where. She *buried* them. I never understood that."

Will stared at me a moment, then followed my gaze to the house.

"My parents are easier," he said quietly.

I let out a breath of dark laughter. "Because they're dead?"

His lips quirked up in a humorless smile. "It's the living you need to worry about..."

We stood there a moment longer, staring in the direction of my cabin. Then headed off slowly down the street—unnoticed in the new-found bustle and commotion.

The arrival of the soldiers may have been a shock, but once it became clear they were no longer a threat the tiny village embraced them just as sincerely as they'd done the fleeing captives.

Every door was open and every person in Midlark was out on the street. Food was prepared in the market, provisions were gathered and rationed for communal use. It was very similar as to when we'd arrived. Only this time was different. This time they weren't the only ones offering help.

I stopped in my tracks, watching as a middle-aged man cloaked in royal crimson gave a spur of the moment tutorial to a boy standing in front of him, waving a borrowed sword. The boy's mother was sitting on the front porch of a nearby cottage, sipping cider from a calfskin flask. The kind of thing you couldn't get in the mountains. The kind of thing that came from the capital.

"They brought a lot with them," Will commented, watching the same thing. "A lot of food, a lot of supplies. A lot of weapons, too...not that we have much idea how to use them."

The swords clashed in the distance, then one clattered to the ground.

No, the palace taught us different things.

We stood there watching as the battle continued in slow-motion. The soldier was patient, even kind, as he guided the youngster's movements. Taking him through the steps, pausing every now and then to adjust his stance and explain the footwork.

I'd seen similar things from my window at the palace. The guards stationed there didn't typically run through drills, but there were times the commander would take new recruits through basic exercises in the open space behind the gardens.

How much more skilled those soldiers looked, how confident and practiced. I shuddered to think any one of them squaring off against the boy with the sword. Then again, some of those same soldiers had come to join us. Some of that talent was now aligned with our side.

"We need to figure this out," Will murmured, eyes locked upon the cheerful duel. "I had expected the people to rally towards us, not the soldiers. If we could get an entire battalion..."

He trailed off and I stole a glance at his face.

While my own thoughts had yet to progress past the arrival of my father, he was staring at the troops with an expression I hadn't seen since that first night he spoke of leaving the palace.

If I wasn't mistaken, it bordered on hope.

"You think we can win?" I asked flatly.

I hadn't intended to sound so cynical. When he flinched, I felt a pang of guilt. But my own outlook had darkened somewhat after stumbling into the woods. Much as I was pleased for the boost in morale, the clattering of swords conjured nothing but chilling memories. And I didn't see what good even an entire battalion would do against the weight of the royal army.

That army rode with Eric into battle. That army has already taken countless lives.

"I think we can make it an unappealing fight," he answered quietly, unwilling to meet my gaze. "By starving them of supplies and rallying those people already at the furthest reaches of their control...I think perhaps we can force some kind of compromise."

I glanced at him in surprise; he'd never spoken like this before.

"A compromise," I repeated. "What might that look like?"

He stared at the troops for a moment, then shrugged.

"I don't know. Maybe they would agree to end the claiming. Maybe they would agree to let the provinces keep more of their own resources, reduce the royal presence. At this point, if they would simply agree not to let us starve—"

"You've *never* spoken like this before," I interrupted, turning to face him. The swords were still clattering behind us, but I stared directly into his eyes. "You've talked about us marching all together towards the capital, meeting them on the field of battle. The people of Nimoa have already driven them back. We sent Joseph and the others to Bunkhill just to get the explosives—"

"And then Joseph and the others were killed," he said bluntly. "Where do you think those explosives ended up? Those warships they reclaimed in Nimoa won't help us on the battlefield; the most they can do is sustain a blockade. And as for the people we've rallied..."

There was a final metallic *clang* as the boy's sword fell to the ground.

"I know it's not what we talked about," he said quietly. "I know it's not what Matthew..." A painful silence fell between us. "...but we need to be realistic."

A surge of anger shot through me.

Even though I'd already spiraled past words like compromise into all-out fatalism, even though I'd been watching the soldiers with the same nagging questions myself, I found myself suddenly furious that anyone else would share in my doubts. Let alone channel them into some kind of talking point—something that made sense. Something that might actually affect some change.

"Realistic," I quoted bitterly. "By giving up the fight—"

"By redefining what it means to win."

Those dark eyes held mine tenderly, but there wasn't a hint of apology. Quite the opposite. He reached for my fingers—giving them a coaxing squeeze.

"You just got your parents back," he said softly. "I just got my sister. And we just got some actual soldiers to stand alongside us—with a hope that more might come our way. This is all good news, Elise. This is all progress. *Leverage.* But to force things into an actual fight?"

He quieted a moment, then shook his head.

"No, I don't think we can win."

I LEFT THE VILLAGE shortly after, wandering by myself through the woods.

Soon after Will's and my rather unsettling conversation, my parents had reemerged from the cabin and began glancing covertly around the square—perhaps to seek their reluctant daughter. I'd taken a single look, then fled into the forest without a moment's pause.

Family reconciliation and palace negotiations. Tenuous compromises all around.

I had faith in none of it.

The second I lost sight of those thatched roofs, it became easier to breathe. The clamoring of swords and quick clip of conversation gave way to the gentler sounds of the forest—the descant whistling of invisible birds, a pine-scented wind rippling through a thousand newly-formed leaves.

After a few secluded minutes I stopped just to take it in, tilting my face to the heavens as my arms drifted out by my sides. I'd done the same thing since I was just a little girl, imagining how it might feel to spontaneously take flight, soaring away from Midlark and up into the clouds—

Twang.

My arms dropped immediately as my head spun in the opposite direction. There weren't many things in the world that made such a precise sound. As a daughter of the mountains, I knew the sharp pluck of a bowstring when I heard it. I just didn't know where it was coming from—

Twang.

This time, I actually saw it—the slice of an arrow as it streaked through the trees.

Without stopping to consider whether it might be a foolish idea, I ventured closer. Picking my way through the dense underbrush until I came to the edge of a clearing.

There was a target on one side. Remy was holding a bow on the other.

Every few seconds, he'd nock an arrow to the string.

Twang.

"You're a good shot."

He jumped in his skin, almost dropping the bow entirely. Bright eyes scanned the tree-line, but he didn't see me until I stepped out with a faint smile.

"I thought you'd never used one of those before."

He'd said as much back at the palace—during my dreaded engagement festivities, wherein the preening members of the court dressed in their woodland finery and prepared for a hunt.

It had seemed utterly ridiculous at the time. A bit more ominous now.

"I hadn't," he answered shortly, turning back to the target. There were a few arrows littered in the surrounding grass, but for the most part he'd buried them in the center rings. "I asked one of the soldiers if I could borrow one to practice. Been working on it ever since."

For the first time, I wondered how long I'd been unconscious. The sun had just newly risen when I was in the garden. Now, it was already beginning to sink into the later hours of the day.

I nodded silently, coming to stand by his side.

We hadn't talked much since the flood. He hadn't talked much to anybody. I'd seen both Zadie and Demetrius trying to engage him, but both were politely shut down.

"You're good," I repeated quietly as he released another arrow. "When we finally return to the palace...I should stand next to you."

Not that we can win such a fight. Not that some of us don't even want to fight.

He made a quiet sound, almost like a laugh. "That's the last place you want to be standing."

Another arrow—this one buried in the grass.

I watched as he moved forward to recover it, refilling the borrowed quiver with fingers so pale I wondered why he hadn't brought a cloak. He yanked each one loose with quick, robotic movements before sweeping back to start the process all over again.

Twang.

"Don't be ridiculous," I said with forced lightness, stealing an arrow from the quiver and tapping it against my hand. "You could save me."

He took it without looking, lifting it to the string. "I can't save anyone," he said quietly. "I couldn't save her."

Twang.

I froze beside him, looking straight ahead. At this point I didn't know if he was talking about the countess or the servant girl who'd fallen into the water.

Knowing Remy, it was probably both.

"You went back for the girl," I murmured, hesitant to upset him further. "You were the only one who did. Just like you jumped without thinking to save Ella. Just like you tackled that guard in Nimoa to rescue Zadie. Just like you ran straight through an enemy camp to save Will and me."

Twang.

I placed a gentle hand on his arm, forcing him to meet my gaze.

"You save people, Remy."

His lovely face tightened, choking on all those things he couldn't say. Then he tore his eyes away from mine—staring back down the mountain the way we came.

"Not everyone," he breathed. "Not her."

I could still feel the thunder making my shoes shake. I could still hear him screaming her name.

But to remember only the moment of the countess' death was to miss the larger picture. A woman who delighted in bloodshed had honored a fallen prisoner. A woman as cold as the alpine streams had thawed to the point of melting. Had thawed to the point of saving an innocent life.

"...I think you did."

Twang.

He reached for another arrow, only to realize they were all gone. Instead of going after them he stood there, staring blankly at the target. The minutes slipped past, quiet and uncounted.

Then, after a long while, he turned back to me.

"Is it true you tripped over a tree branch?"

I stiffened involuntarily, glancing back towards the village.

"I fainted."

As if that makes it any better.

"Now I'm hiding out here from my mother, who seems inconveniently determined to love me, and my father...who's been serving in the queen's guard."

Remy froze in shock, staring at me. After a few seconds, he offered me the bow.

Chapter 13

It was getting dark by the time we returned to the village.

The communal supper had ended and most of the children had been banished inside. Many of their parents had voluntarily joined them, but a few lingered with the soldiers in the center of the square. A fire was blazing, and hushed voices caught and carried on the breeze.

Our friends were near the center, looking a bit overwhelmed.

Those voices were bouncing back and forth, carrying on half a dozen conversations. Most were directed at them, but there seemed to be very little rhyme or reason as to what was being said.

"—done well to start recruiting in Nimoa," one of the troops was saying. "They're already beginning to feel the shortages. Two shipments of grain were supposed to have traveled to the capital. Another was scheduled to arrive the week we left. Nothing ever came—"

"—cutting food rations, lines in the capital village just to buy bread. The valley itself supplies such a limited stream of produce, it can't possibly last—"

"—munitions would have helped. You were wise to send people there as well. But after our people intercepted those returning from Bunkhill, I'm afraid the expedition was for naught—"

"But what of the troops?" Zadie asked, not for the first time. A lone woman standing amidst a sea of men, nearly lost in the clamor, but I caught the bright glint of her hair. "The ones stationed at the base of the mountain. Some were killed by the flood, but the rest of the company—"

"The rest of the company is no longer a concern," a deep voice interrupted.

I stiffened in surprise to see my father standing at the center of the crowd, just across the fire from my friends. There was nothing particularly commanding about his presence, as all the soldiers looked and dressed the same. But the others quieted when he spoke, listening attentively.

Remy shot me a quick glance, then lifted a reassuring hand to my back.

"So many troops deserted that the remaining army is going back to the capital," he continued, staring across the flames at Will. "After what happened in Nimoa, I would suspect they wish to regroup in the royal valley, assess their numbers and see where they stand."

The words themselves were lost on me; I couldn't get past the sound of his voice. How had he been taken? How had he been returned? It felt like just yesterday, but lifetimes had passed.

You've grown up, cricket.

"So we've been given a reprieve," someone shouted from the back. "If the troops have been recalled, they cannot influence what happens next."

A ripple of conversation agitated the group.

"What do you mean?" Zadie asked in confusion. "It is merely a postponement—"

"You cannot truly mean to *fight* the royal army," another soldier interrupted. "I don't care how many people have defected, it would be a slaughter—nothing more."

Will glanced at them, but said nothing. My father never broke his piercing gaze.

"You think the choice is ours?" Demetrius lifted his eyebrows in surprise. "We set fire to the palace and killed half the aristocracy. One way or another, this is ending in a fight—"

"Maybe...maybe not," the soldier pressed. "The blockade is costly and the palace is weak. If their supply lines keep hemorrhaging..."

"He's right," another took up the cause. "If we can keep the pressure on the supplies, their problems will become so great they might no longer concern themselves with ours. We could return to our own provinces, shore up support and govern ourselves."

Another shockwave flew through the group. This was more divisive than the last.

"That will never work," Remy murmured beside me, shaking his head.

The two of us were still standing at the end of the street, loath to come any closer, though the absence of our presence was sorely felt. Isabelle was gone—presumably off caring for a stranger's baby. And Will had been uncharacteristically silent, keeping his opinions to himself.

The only people speaking in defense of our original plan were Demetrius and Zadie, both of whom looked increasingly exasperated to be the only ones doing so.

"That will *never* work," she said flatly, echoing Remy's exact words. "Under no circumstance will the palace simply ignore what we've done. It's only a matter of time—"

A chorus of voices rang up in the darkness, drowning out whatever she said next.

There seemed no end to it. Some people were arguing to stir up opinion, others were trying to keep calm. The soldiers were bad enough, nothing but hot tempers, but the dissent wasn't limited to them alone. What few remained from Joseph's group had been badly shaken by their brush with the royal infantry, and had no desire to encounter them again. My own companions had been thrust yet again into the spotlight, and were struggling under the weight of all those expectant eyes.

"Come on," Remy said quietly, nudging me forward. "We can't leave them alone."

I nodded faintly but held back as he walked towards them, lingering on the edge of the street. It took me a moment to realize I wasn't the only one. A pair of bright eyes was watching from the shadows, flickering every now and then when they caught the light of the flames.

Jane.

"Say something," Demetrius hissed in frustration to Will. "Why do you just stand there?"

He opened his mouth, but fell silent beneath my father's gaze. Twice his eyes swept over the square, quite possibly looking for me, then he finally lifted a hand and cleared his throat.

"Peace, friends! There's enough at stake without us arguing with one another." He waited until the crowd quieted, raising his voice to be heard. "Some of you wish to fight, some wish simply to return home...perhaps there is a middle ground."

My eyes snapped shut as his words echoed back.

Redefine what it means to win.

"A middle ground?" Zadie turned to him in surprise. "This is coming from *you*?"

A faint blush spread across his cheeks, but he nodded swiftly and kept his eyes roving through the crowd. Seeing everyone but focusing on no one in particular.

"Yes, it's coming from me," he answered quietly. "What does that tell you?"

Her eyes flashed in anger. "That you're giving up!"

He stared at her a long moment, then shook his head.

"What would you have me say? We cannot return to our lives as if nothing has happened, but neither can we stand against the royal army and possibly survive. I'm not giving up. I'm saying we need to rethink our strategy if we want to have any chance of walking away from this."

She threw up her hands in disbelief.

"But *everyone* is coming! We've sent people throughout the entire realm, and that was before we even knew about the sentiment of the soldiers! We can overwhelm them with numbers. This is no time to lose faith—"

"I haven't lost faith," he interrupted with a touch of anger. "I'm simply not willing to risk your life on it, Zadie. I'm not willing to risk Elise, or Remy, or my sister, or any of the other people here. Not if there might be another way. If there's even a *chance* that we can negotiate—"

"Negotiate with the palace?!" she cried. "Either your memory has begun to fade, or you are actively trying to forget! We cannot *negotiate* with these people, William. We set a great many of them on fire! Do you think they've forgotten? Do you think they'll be eager to *negotiate* after all that?"

The crowd was splitting into halves, simmering with tension, just waiting to explode.

"And what is your solution?" he snapped back. "A brawl in the middle of the field?"

"You always knew it would come to that!"

"It was a move of desperation, Zadie! I would never have chosen such a thing myself! We are *outmatched* with swords and spears, no matter our numbers! But if we can force an accord—"

"An accord!" She spat the word like it was poison, stepping so close she was nearly standing on his toes. "An accord with the people who tied you to that bed every night. An accord with the people who chased us through the streets of Nimoa. The same people who killed Theo—"

A swarm of angry voices overwhelmed them once again.

Remy had reached the churning crowd and was pushing frantically to the center. My father was calling for silence, while Demetrius tried to hold Zadie and Will back. I took a step forward myself, ready to intercede, when movement at the edge of the firelight caught my attention again.

As the others raged amongst themselves, Jane had slipped away into the shadows—ghosting up the abandoned street. No one else had seen her watching. No one noticed when she was gone.

I froze mid-step, torn by indecision.

I knew what I was supposed to do. I knew what I was supposed to say when I got there. In the dancing light of a village fire, the tenuous rebellion we'd worked so hard to protect was coming apart at the seams.

My friends needed my help. My voice should have been loudest among them.

Yet I couldn't tear my eyes away.

A second later, I was following her. Gliding with a surreal kind of animation, propelled with an impulse I couldn't control. The fire burned like an angry blaze in the backs of my eye, then faded into shadow as we left the village entirely and vanished into the trees.

I DON'T KNOW HOW LONG we were walking, but we couldn't have gone very far. The second those voices faded into silence the girl stopped abruptly, standing on the edge of a wide clearing tucked away within the trees. The grass was bathed in shadow but in the moonlight I could see waves of rippling flowers, their red petals stained silver, stretching as far as the eye could see.

I froze in the darkness behind her, feeling as though I'd stepped into a dream.

"I used to come here all the time," she said quietly, staring across the field. "My parents worked late at the butcher's, so this was my place until sundown. I'd lie in the grass for hours and stare up at the sky. It was always so quiet. The village was too noisy...I could never think."

I took a step closer, staring at the back of her head. At this point I didn't even know how she'd seen me, but none of that mattered now. We were poised at the edge of something greater.

"Jane...why did they bring you to the palace?"

Her shoulders stiffened, but her eyes never left the field. "I'd read sometimes," she murmured. "Not too many books around here, but I took some from the old schoolhouse and brought them with me. Memorized them from cover to cover."

I circled in front of her, stepping into her line of sight.

"Jane—"

Tears were streaming down her cheeks. That pink ribbon flapped in the breeze.

"They're just books," she whispered. "It never hurt anyone to read."

I stared at her for a long time, remembering exactly how she looked as a child. That thin frame was trembling, giving off a spectral shadow that stretched all the way back to the trees.

"What happened at the palace?"

She froze perfectly still, then lifted her eyes to mine.

"IT WAS THE PLAGUE," I said quietly, standing in front of the fire. "That's the secret that was binding the high court together. That's how the palace kept the provinces from rebelling again."

The dust had settled back in the village and most of the people arguing had given up and gone to bed. Only a few remained—all the regular faces, plus a few soldiers. None of them looked like they could believe what they were hearing. Still, they were listening with bated breath.

"I don't understand," Zadie stammered. "They just...they just set it loose?"

Set it loose.

Like it was a wild animal, something to be released from its cage and set upon an unsuspecting land. In hindsight, I supposed that was a frightfully apt way of describing it.

But the worst was yet to come.

"They did more than that...they created it. Jane created it." My eyes strayed down the road to where I'd left her, still crying in the field. "The girl's a genius. An actual genius. When the soldiers came to Midlark, it was clear to see. They took her to the palace, sat her down at a table, asked her questions...she had no idea where any of it was leading. She was just a child."

A frightening look swept across many of their faces, and I wasn't sure any of those qualifiers made the slightest bit of difference. I glanced automatically at Will, but the man was simply stunned.

"How did...?" Remy cleared his throat and tried again. "How did they manage to spread it to so many people? The sickness swept through every province. Nothing was spared."

At this point, it hardly mattered. But I answered all the same.

"They infected the livestock," I echoed the words I'd just heard myself, "shipped them across the realm. When the people ate, they got sick. Too sick to band together. Too sick to fight."

An unthinkable strategy, but it did the job. It had been years, but most of the provinces still hadn't recovered. They were scattered and disorganized, easily subjected to royal rule.

The price of a crown. This one cost your very soul.

A horrible silence swept over them, gripping soldiers, captives, and villagers alike. Such a thing was too much to process through a belated discussion. Too much for one little group of people standing in front of a fire. No matter which way they approached, their minds went blank.

And still...the question remained.

"But that isn't right," Will said suddenly, lifting his eyes to mine. An uncertain emotion made him hesitate before the words came spilling out. "You said nothing was spared...but the sickness never came to Midlark. Death swept over the entire realm...but life here remained the same."

It was the exact same thing I'd said to Jane only a few minutes before. A final twisting of the knife that left me utterly speechless when she finally confessed.

"That part was planned as well," I replied softly. "You remember the flower I showed you in the garden? Those vibrant red petals—I told you it was native in these parts?"

He nodded mutely and I pulled in a breath.

"In the flower lies the immunity. There was no curse, no blessing—none of the stories we told ourselves were true. Just a simple flower. In Midlark, we breathed it in every single day."

According to Jane, it was the natural balance of things. For every poison, there was an antidote. For every act of evil, a tiny act of good to tip the scales.

My entire life, everyone had assumed it was a quirk of geography. That the village was too remote and high in the mountains for such sickness to spread. But as it turned out, the plague hadn't spared Midlark after all. We were the beginning and the end. And everything in between.

"She never told anyone?" my mother asked in a hushed voice. She was standing rigid beside my father, leaning against him in a way I don't think she was aware of herself. "Not anyone?"

"They would kill her," I said shortly. "If anyone knew, they would kill her on the spot."

Despite all that had happened, it was a fact that weighed heavy on my mind.

Even by telling this small group of people, I was actively risking the girl's life. There wasn't a family in the realm who hadn't been touched by such darkness. It was the kind of scar that never faded, one that had been too deeply felt. There would be cries of vengeance, cries for blood.

But terrible as the story was, it hadn't finished just yet.

My gaze circled slowly around the fire, resting a moment on each face. When I spoke, the words were slow and deliberate—chosen in the darkness as I made my way back through the trees.

"It's how they beat us...and it's how we can beat them."

A group of blank faces stared back at me.

"What are you talking about?" Demetrius asked faintly. Despite having grown up in a nearby crest of mountains, the plague had descended upon his village all the same. "It is a blasphemy, what the girl did. A sin for which there is no reprieve. Yet you wish for her to conjure up the same kind of evil? Unleash that same hell upon the land?"

I shook my head slowly, avoiding one particular set of eyes. "There's no need for conjuring...that evil never left the palace."

THE PLAN WAS SIMPLE.

While the rest of our rebellion assembled in the royal valley Jane and I would sneak into the palace, steal back the darkness she'd created, and unleash it upon those who'd used it before.

Poetic justice aside, it happened to be the perfect solution to all our problems.

The trouble with the volatile arguments raging around the fire was that each one of those shouting voices had been right. There was no way to win such a fight, and there was no way to avoid it. There was also no way to reach a compromise, desperate wishing aside. That left only one option.

To stand against the palace...and win.

But not everyone felt the same way.

"You cannot do this to me!"

Will had stood by in silence when I shared my plan with the others. He'd nodded along when I spoke of turning the enemy's weapon against them. He'd grimaced when I'd explained the process of slipping into the palace unseen, but he recognized the necessity of it.

Then I said that I'd be the one going. And everything had fallen apart.

"We can't keep having the same argument," I murmured, rubbing my eyes as the sun peeked over the distant mountains. "We've been going in circles all night. Nothing's going to change—"

Two strong hands gripped my arms, pulling me back to my feet.

"And we will *keep* having the same argument until you see reason!"

The news of my involvement hadn't gone over well, least of all with my parents—who flew into such a frenzy that a pair of soldiers took it upon themselves to lead them gently away. The second they were gone, Remy and Demetrius rounded on me. They were just building up steam, when Zadie pushed through the center and slapped me across the face.

But none of them held a candle to Will.

Without stopping to say a word to anyone, he grabbed me by the arm and dragged me straight into the forest—ironically coming to a stop in the very same meadow where Jane had made her moonlight confession just a few hours before.

I thought he'd have relented by now. At the very least, I'd hoped the long hours would have caught up with him and he'd have simply fallen asleep. But I'd clearly underestimated him.

The man was just getting warmed up.

"How would you feel in my position?" he insisted, holding on tighter when I tried to pull away. "Would you let me walk into the palace, straight into the arms of all those people we've been trying to evade? The same people who *hanged* us from those very walls. Would you let me do that?"

I might realize it wasn't my decision to make.

"Someone has to do this—"

"But that someone doesn't have to be you," he insisted, pulling me closer. "If this is really the only way, then let me do it. I can go with Jane. We'll find whatever it is she's looking for and be back before anyone—"

"You really think that's a better idea?" I said quietly, repeating the same argument I'd made a dozen times before. "You're really going to pretend that makes sense?"

"It makes more sense than you—"

"I can disguise myself!" I cried, finally losing my temper. "I can wear the gown of a servant. I can dye my eyes and cover my hair. Such things are customary for a woman. What would you do, Will? Put on some pale robes and walk in with your head held high? They would arrest you before you'd made it past the throne room—that's *if* they didn't kill you first!"

"Then let it be someone else," he shot back. "If it must be a woman, then let it be any other woman in the camp. You have done *enough*, Elise. This doesn't have to fall on you."

"Listen to what you're saying," I chided gently, trying to calm him down. "We are both symbols, you and I. We are the spark that started this, and we must see it through to the end. It might not be fair, but it's the choice we made that night. You, me, and Matthew—"

Will shook his head, looking as though I'd set him on fire.

"You wish to sacrifice yourself as he did, to give your life to the cause." His eyes burned into mine, refusing to release me. "But your life is not what's needed. These people need you to survive. *I* need you to survive. I don't care if it's easier to play the martyr—"

"*Easier?*" I cried, finally incensed. "Of all the paths set before us in the days to come, you think I've chosen the one that's *easier*—"

"Matthew died," he said shortly. "All his troubles are over. Is that what you want?"

I pulled away from him, feeling as though I'd been stung. "...that's a terrible thing to say."

He stared back without feeling, a cold statue in the fading night. "There's a fine line between sacrifice and suicide. Matthew understood it. But you? The heart of this revolution walking through the palace doors? I'm not sure that you do."

I stepped right in front of him, staring into his eyes. "It is *because* I'm the heart of this revolution that I need to walk through those doors. The people we've assembled are risking their lives. They need to see me do that."

When he looked away, I caught him lightly by the chin.

"And who knows...it might work out perfectly." I tilted my head, trying to coax a little smile. "If it doesn't, we can always tell people I tripped over a tree."

He pulled out of reach, staring down with a dark expression. "...are you making jokes about this?"

I glanced down with a sigh, sweeping back my hair and tying it in a little bun. "I'm not." I stifled a yawn, too exhausted to play our game any longer. The entire night had slipped past us, and the sun was already rising in a new dawn. "I'm scared and tired. I just want to sleep."

The man couldn't care less that I was tired, but it caught him off guard when I confessed to being afraid. Without another word he sank into the grass at the base of a tall oak tree, opening his arms for me to lie down beside him. I considered for a fraction of a second, trying to determine whether he meant to continue badgering me, then decided I was too tired to care.

Let him talk, I thought wearily, sinking down beside him. *Perhaps he'll talk himself to sleep.*

The air was chilled, but he was somehow warm in spite of it. With a silent breath of contentment, I curled into a catlike ball—closing my eyes and resting my cheek against his shirt.

Strange that it had become so easy to sleep outside. Despite having been raised in relative squalor, my parents had made absolutely sure that I always had a roof over my head. It had taken some time to adjust to something different. Now, I scarcely noticed it at all.

"Elise—"

"No," I interrupted quickly, refusing to open my eyes. "You're done, Will. I gave you the entire night—it was an enormous mistake and I'd rather be dreaming. Go to sleep, or I'll kill you."

I couldn't see his face, but his chest shook with silent laughter.

"I'm rethinking this whole 'falling in love with you' bit. Perhaps I'd like someone nicer."

"That's fantastic," I mumbled, pressing my face into his chest. "Let me know when you find her. I'll give her a courtesy warning...and a knife."

He chuckled again, twirling a finger around the little curls that had escaped my bun. "You never wear it like this," he murmured, playing with it gently. "I like it."

I nodded blindly. "Perhaps the new girl will have curls as well."

We lay in silence for a little while, just long enough that I was finally starting to drift away, then he spoke up once again. Gentle, this time. Nothing more than a murmur.

"I didn't mean to taunt you about Matthew. As long as I breathe, I'll never be out of his debt. It's just...you frighten me sometimes. Sometimes I wish you weren't so brave."

I lifted my head incredulously, only to see him staring down with a sad smile. "You must be joking. I'm scared all the time."

He shrugged a little, shifting me higher in his arms. "But you don't let it stop you. You don't let it govern you. You do what you must, and you help others do the same." He gave me another wistful smile. "You're the bravest person I know."

I didn't know what to say to this. Ironically enough, Matthew had penned those same words to me in his letter. *I never knew a girl so brave.* Yet I would never describe myself in such a way.

"Elise...I need you *not* to be brave. I need to keep you." He forced a tight smile, trying to lighten the mood, but an errant tear slipped down his cheek. "Let someone else be brave just this once instead. I won't love you any less. I won't—"

"Will—"

"I need to keep you," he said again, resting a silencing finger upon my lips. "I've never asked for much in this world. I'd never expected to receive anything. Where I come from, moments of joy are so few and far between I never assumed I'd get anything different. But to have collided with a person like you? To have kissed you...held you in my arms..."

He shook his head silently, running a finger down the length of my face.

"I promise, I'll make you happy. You won't regret your decision, just *please*...don't go inside that place. Not if I can't go with you. I couldn't...I couldn't bear it if you didn't come back."

I sucked in a quick breath, trying to keep myself steady.

For as different as our worlds had been, for all the staggering things working against us, we had found a perfect counterpoint in one another. As unlikely as it was strong, a cosmic pull that defied both history and distance. Just a few months we'd known each other, yet his influence carried back to every previous part. As if I'd been simply waiting, not yet realizing it myself.

There was a split second that I wavered. A split second that I allowed myself to imagine how it might feel to simply head into the woods together. To leave the fight for someone else and spend every morning for the rest of my life waking up in the circle of his arms.

Just a perfect, fleeting moment...then it passed.

"I must."

His lips parted, but I held up a quick hand.

"You said it yourself...I do what I must."

He leaned his head against the tree in quiet surrender, staring up at the sky.

A sunrise in the mountains wasn't quite like any other place on earth. Each new dawn was a resurrection—beneath a painted sky, the entire world came back to life. Flowers opened and animals ventured out of their homes. Birds looped in little ribbons, calling out across the endless sky.

"...marry me."

I blinked quickly, plummeting back to earth. "What?"

His entire body went rigid, like he couldn't believe he'd said the words himself. A look of sheer terror flashed through his eyes, and I swear even the birds went silent.

He couldn't have meant it. This can't be real.

"Say that you'll marry me."

I peeled myself off him, turning with a look of bewilderment. He didn't appear to be joking. I didn't appear to be dreaming. Yet even now he was doing the strangest thing.

The terror had vanished, and a spark of life had returned. And his face, that beautiful face I knew almost as well as my own, had melted into a breathtaking smile.

"If you truly must go, then leave me with that promise." He leaned forward, shifting onto his knees in the tall grass. "Something real between us. Something to bring you back home."

Home...did I even know where that was? Hadn't I left one home, only to find myself rocketing towards another? Or maybe I'd been wrong since the beginning.

Maybe that home had been in front of me the whole time.

"I'm not talking about today or tomorrow," he said quietly, tracing the delicate lines of my hand. "But someday. Maybe in a few months, a few years. Will you marry me, Elise?"

My heart was pounding in my ears. I couldn't seem to pull in a breath.

When I finally did manage to speak, it wasn't at all what I'd planned to say.

"I don't want you to ask me like this."

Silence.

A trace of that fear returned and he dropped his eyes with a blush. Our fingers were still entwined, but they burned under a sudden spotlight. One in particular.

"I'm sorry," he murmured, still unable to look at me. "I wasn't planning on..." A shaky breath. "I know you deserve much better. I'll save everything I can for a ring—"

"No," I knelt quickly beside him, clinging desperately to his hands, "I meant like *this*." A furious blush colored my cheeks, burning in the pale light of the rising sun. "Out of desperation, a day before we march on the palace. Because...because you think we might die."

He stared at me a moment, then let out a sudden burst of laughter.

"You think *that's* why I'm asking?" The idea was so ridiculous, for a few seconds he forgot to be afraid. "Elise...I was always going to ask you. I wanted to ask you from the moment I first laid eyes on you. The moment I saw you on the train."

My initial reply vanished in a burst of shock.

"...you remember that?"

In a fuzzy kind of haze, the image came back to me. The downward tilt of his body, dragged between two guards. The sharp crack of the commander's knuckles across his face—punishment for attempting to start a riot. And those fierce, staggering eyes. It was the first time I'd seen them.

But I hadn't thought they'd seen me.

"How did you even..." I trailed off, shaking my head in astonishment. "You were manacled and bleeding. Did you even see me—"

"I saw your shoes."

I smiled in spite of myself, but my eyes were full of tears. "Will—"

"From the moment I saw you," he said again quietly, staring deep into my eyes, "from the moment we danced in the hall. Every single day since then, I have dreamed of nothing else."

His fingers tightened and he took in a faltering breath.

"Will you marry me, Elise?"

The sun broke over the mountains. Slowly at first, then all at once. Sweeping down from the heavens and painting the world in that fledgling, golden glow.

Our eyes met in the middle of it, reflective and wide.

"Yes."

Chapter 14

There was no way to celebrate such news. This was no time for a celebration. We'd sat beneath the tree a while longer, kissing and talking and generally just smiling our heads off, before wandering back to a village in hard transition.

Half the people were packing. The other half was begging them not to go.

"—can't believe you're serious."

I froze mid-step beside Will. *Not* the people I'd thought would be begging.

The two of us paused upon reaching one of the furthest cabins, unseen by two of our closest friends arguing on the other side. Unlike the rest of the village, this wasn't about whether or not to fight—that had already been determined. It was about what might happen in the days to come.

"I'm not trying to upset you," Demetrius insisted, raking back his dark hair. "I'm just trying to be honest. My situation isn't...as free as yours. I have fewer options."

I didn't need to see Zadie's face to guess her exact expression.

"Isn't as free?" she repeated dangerously. "If this is about your daughter, I love the girl to pieces. There isn't a thing in this world that would—"

"Zadie..."

"Let me finish," she demanded. "I couldn't care less that you already have a child. She's your family. I'm only asking for a chance to—"

"I have a wife," he interrupted softly.

There was a weighted pause.

"Not really—" she began.

"But legally. How could I..." He trailed off, looking as desolate as I'd ever seen. "Zadie, I don't know how that would be possible."

Will and I gave each other a quick look, then slipped secretly past them to the street.

We'll give that some space...

Considering its size, the rest of the village was a wild flurry of preparation. Weapons were checked, oiled, and sheathed. Strips of meat were being hastily dried over a fire. Remy was standing with a group of soldiers in the center of the village square—poring over what looked like a map with a thoughtful frown. Every now and then, he'd catch an expectant look and nod swiftly.

Remy—who couldn't plot a course to save his life.

"You should probably head over there," I advised, fighting back a smile. "Before they put him in charge of directions and we find ourselves marching straight back to the sea."

Will laughed softly, then kissed me on the forehead. "This from a girl who thought that 'up' and 'north' were the same thing—"

"Are you going to tell anyone?" I interrupted with sudden interest, simultaneously asking myself the same thing. In a perfect world, I'd run straight to Zadie—but the girl wasn't having the easiest conversation, and the sanctity of marital vows wouldn't be high on her list.

"No," he scoffed. "Of course not."

I raised my eyebrows slowly, and he flashed a mischievous grin.

"Yes. I'm going to tell everyone." The playful twinkle dimmed somewhat as his eyes swept over the street. "But afterwards...not now. Not when it's like this."

I understood this perfectly, thinking the same thing myself. That being said, I found myself caught completely off guard when he asked the same question.

"Are you going to tell your parents?"

I wanted to dismiss it outright—citing the same 'world hangs in the balance' timing, but it wasn't exactly the same thing. His only remaining family was back in Reeves, but mine was literally a stone's throw away. And while I could only assume my father would be coming with us, my mother was staying in the village. If I didn't tell her now...there might not be another chance.

Will I even come back to Midlark when this is over? Whenever I dream of the future, it's always been Will and me living together somewhere by the sea...

"After," I echoed after a brief deliberation. He gave me the same pointed look, and I raised my hands with a grin. "I will—I promise. If we come back alive, I'll tell the whole world."

He tensed in spite of himself, but covered it with a quick smile. "There it is...that sparkling sense of humor."

I grinned again, biting my lower lip. "I still can't believe this is happening. It feels like something out of a dream."

It felt like a betrayal to be excited, especially considering the circumstances. But every time my thoughts started turning towards the palace, I found myself back under that blissful little tree.

Seize these moments while you can. Jokes aside, it's likely there won't be many left.

"You won't be able to keep it to yourself," I added matter-of-factly. "You won't last ten seconds around Remy."

"Oh you of little faith," he countered, walking off with a little wink.

I started heading in the opposite direction, then glanced back to see for myself.

He had reached the troops and took his place alongside them, staring dutifully at the map. A second later, his foot started tapping. Then his lips twitched with a secret grin. A second after that, he leaned over and whispered something into Remy's ear.

Remy nodded along distractedly, then turned with a sudden, "What?!"

Called it.

With a rather superior smile, I found myself wandering along the street—doing my best not to look happy, watching the frantic commotion, noting with detached interest that despite having returned to my childhood home, I had nothing to pack. I was so caught up in my own thoughts, I didn't hear Isabelle calling until she grabbed my arm.

"What's the matter with you, Midlark? Are you drunk?"

I blinked in surprise, then yanked myself free. "...motherhood looks good on you."

For the first time since I'd met her, the stunning girl had lost a bit of her usual shine. Her hair was matted, her clothes were disheveled, and there were dark shadows under4 her eyes.

That being said, she looked...happy?

So there are at least three of us.

"Yeah, about that..." She glanced at the ground, two bright spots of color reddening her cheeks. "It isn't as random as you think. I knew her mother...a little."

I nodded faintly, but said nothing.

In truth, the two girls could have been perfect strangers and the baby would still be better for it. Orphaned children didn't last long in our world. It was good she had someone to care for her.

I had just been blown away that Isabelle was the one to volunteer.

"I'd just been looking for a reason, you know?" she continued suddenly, pawing at the dirt with her toe. "Such terrible things couldn't just happen...there had to be some kind of master plan."

...are YOU drunk?

"That's a bit of wishful thinking," I said delicately, uncertain how to proceed. "You and I both know that terrible things happen every day without meaning or cause—"

"Not these kinds of things," she interrupted quietly. "What happened at the palace..." Her gaze lifted, staring into the distant sky. "It couldn't be senseless. There had to be *something.*"

For the second time, I found myself on unfamiliar ground. Isabelle was one of the darkest, most hilariously cynical people I knew. To hear her waxing philosophical?

"So that's the reason you took the baby?" I asked hesitantly.

She glanced up suddenly, like she'd forgotten I was there.

"No," she said shortly. "You were right. Terrible things happen every day. There is no sense or reason." She paused a moment before adding, "But that child needed a protector."

So maybe we'll call it a draw.

"At any rate, it's perfect timing." She tried to toss back her hair before realizing it was in a messy knot at the back of her head. "Just in time for me to return to the palace...and die."

My eyebrows shot up in surprise.

"You're coming with us? What about—"

"She'll be in good hands," she interrupted lightly. "She's staying with your mother until I get back. I'm pretty sure Ella's going to be there, too."

...my mother?!

I pushed back the initial shock and focused on something smaller instead.

"Oh, well that's...I'm just surprised. You've never come with us before."

It had always seemed a glaring inconsistency in her personality, but it was true. The trading village in the mountains, the tavern in Nimoa...the girl always pushed ahead, then stayed behind.

"That's because I didn't have anything to come back to," she said simply. "I guess I didn't trust myself not to do something reckless. If my life was the only thing at stake..." She trailed off a few seconds then warmed with a sudden smile. "But now I have someone. I have Lissie."

I tilted my head, smiling in return. "Lissie?"

There was an almost guilty pause.

"...Lissium." She shot me a worried look. "Too dark?"

The antidote to our poison. The realm's only hope.

"I'd expect nothing less."

The two of us shared another quick smile, the kind that held more affection than either of us was prepared to admit. Then we headed off in separate directions.

It wasn't until I'd already crossed the street that I turned suddenly back around.

"Izzy...Will and I are getting married."

Her face lightened with a look of surprise, even the hint of a smile when she saw my uncontrollable grin. Then, as quickly as it happened, she darkened with a scowl.

"That's the meanest thing you've ever said to me."

THE REST OF THE DAY passed quickly, and by the time the sun began to sink once more towards the trees the preparations were complete and we were ready to depart.

"It's fewer people than we thought," Will said quietly, finding me across the square and coming to stand by my side. "The plague was a double-edged sword. Many think it's the only way we can win, but others are using it as an excuse. Saying that if everything goes as planned, there won't be any need for a fight at all. No need for them to come along."

And if everything doesn't go as planned?

"That's all right," I answered more confidently than I felt. "They said it themselves. If Jane's right about the remaining vials, there won't be a need for them after all."

He glanced down at the top of my head. "...right."

There weren't many lingering farewells, just a few amongst the people of the village. The soldiers had been traveling together for months and were grimly accustomed to the idea they might never return. The only dissonance was amongst the captives, many of whom desired to stay.

"Have you said goodbye to your mother?" Will asked softly, watching as a girl who'd been captured with the group in Bunkhill covered her face and sobbed. "There's still time."

I shifted uneasily, glancing towards my house.

"She isn't..." My breath hitched and I shook my head. "I haven't seen her." Before he could say anything, I added quickly, "Did you know she volunteered to watch the children?"

He nodded in silence. "That was sweet of her."

I scoffed, tightening the clasp on my cloak. "*Sweet*. I might have chosen a different word."

He glanced at me again, lips twitching with the hint of a smile. "I was under the impression you two had found some common ground."

My eyes strayed past the house towards a group of soldiers. One soldier in particular.

"We found a common enemy, and that's not the same thing."

At that moment, the front door opened and the woman in question wandered onto the porch. Sure enough, there was baby sleeping in the living room behind her. Ella had already bid a tearful farewell to her father and was being bounced quietly on her hip.

"She's looking for you," Will murmured as her eyes scanned worriedly over the street. "If it was me—"

"Yes, but it *isn't* you," I interrupted curtly. "You said it yourself—your parents are easier."

He stifled a rueful grin. "How very convenient for you. Glad they could help."

The two of us shared a quick look before turning back to the square.

The last of the provisions were packed. The weapons were sheathed. Packs were being hitched onto shoulders. After all these weeks of wandering, the time was finally upon us.

"Will!" Remy called, weaving to the front of the group. "Are you guys ready?"

I took a step towards them, but Will held up a finger.

"One last thing."

His fingers locked around my wrist. And before I knew what was happening, he was dragging me cheerfully backwards—waving to my mother as we approached the house.

"I hope you won't mind if *I* say a quick goodbye." He flashed her another breathtaking smile, speaking through his teeth. "The woman is going to be my mother-in-law, after all."

My cheeks went cold and I dug in my heels.

"That could *so easily* change—"

"Thank you again for agreeing to watch the children." He pulled us to a stop in front of the porch, flicking Ella beneath the chin and giving my mother a quick kiss on the cheek. "It was a pleasure to meet you. I'm sure we'll be seeing you again very soon."

Traitor.

"It was a pleasure to meet you as well," she said slowly, glancing between us. "I'm sorry we didn't get more time."

Too late now. He'll be dead by sundown. I'm going to kill him.

"What's that?" He cupped a hand to his ear with a look of confusion. "I'm sorry—Remy's calling me. You two finish up here and I'll meet Elise up front."

Both my mother and I watched as he lifted a hand in farewell and jogged lightly across the street towards the others. Her eyes twinkled with amusement. Mine were narrowed in silent rage.

"He's not very subtle, is he?"

I ground my teeth together. "No, he's not."

An awkward silence fell between us, one made all the worse when Ella hopped down from her arms and ran off to bid her father a final farewell. I considered taking off right after her before remembering I didn't have the excuse of being four. Instead, I turned to my mother with a soft sigh.

"That being said, he's right. It *is* very kind of you to watch the children. Thank you for that." I tucked my hair nervously behind my ears, stepping back. "I'm sure we'll be—"

"I haven't reconciled with your father."

My head jerked up in surprise.

It had been a question I'd been too afraid to ask. The return of one parent had been jarring enough; I hadn't known what to do with the second. And when they shut themselves in the house?

"...you didn't?"

She shook her head slowly, eyes shining with unshed tears.

"Not yet. Too much has happened, too much time has passed. He and I might get there one day, but for now..." She trailed off, staring towards the soldiers.

There were lines on her face I hadn't remembered. Many more lines than had been there before. I stared at them for a moment, counting the tiny wrinkles, then abruptly took her hand.

"I'm going to come back. This plan of ours is going to work, and I'm going to come back." I hesitated a moment before squeezing her fingers. "And then Will and I are moving to Nimoa. We want to get married and live by the sea...and I want you to come with us."

Her face drained of all color, frozen in surprise.

"You do?"

I do?

I nodded with sudden determination.

"Yes, I do."

There was a second when I thought she was going to break down. A second when I thought she would lose all composure and cry. She didn't. She embraced me instead.

A soft gasp escaped my lips as I was pulled into those arms I used to know so well. Closing my eyes and leaning into them like I was a child, I breathed in that soft, familiar scent.

"I would like that very much."

I let out a watery laugh, sniffing secretly at her hair, then pulled back with a smile.

The two of us stared at each other for a suspended moment. She reached out and tucked a stray curl behind my ears. Then I lifted my hand in farewell and headed off towards the others.

I hadn't made it halfway there before she called out quietly.

"Elise...I haven't reconciled with your father. But I allowed him to explain." Her eyes locked on mine. "I hope you'll give him that same chance."

IT WASN'T A LONG JOURNEY back to the royal valley, not considering how far our travels had already taken us. Time passed even more quickly without the fear of hunger and discovery that had plagued us since the first time we left the valley, venturing into the wilderness beyond.

The days passed quickly and we fell into a simple rhythm—hiking in the day, hunting in the evening, setting up camp at nightfall, and continuing forward with every new dawn. Sometimes, the soldiers would give us lessons. If everything went as planned there would be no need for weapons, but the closer we got to the palace the more we found ourselves wanting to pick up a blade.

Remy went out each evening after we'd stopped and practiced with his bow. I never found out who'd lent it to him, but he apparently didn't have the heart to take it back. Some days, Will would go with him—retrieving the arrows as they spoke in hushed voices about what was to come. Some days, I would go with them as well—anything to avoid the growing tension in the camp. Anything to avoid the eyes of my father, which followed me wherever I decided to go.

It was one of these evenings, when we were only a day's journey from the palace, that I decided to leave the camp behind and venture into the woods to find them.

My father had been staring more relentlessly than usual, probably building himself up for a last-minute speech before we all marched off to meet our fate. I didn't want to be anywhere in the vicinity when that happened so, when he was distracted by one of his companions, I picked up a spare quiver and headed off into the trees.

It was warm, unseasonably warm, but that's what they liked in the capital. A balmy lack of seasons. Sunshine and a convenient absence of rain.

We're close enough to feel their weather.

I glanced up at the sky with a shiver, then quickened my pace—almost running into Demetrius when he swept the opposite way down the trail.

"Careful," he admonished as he caught me gently. "Are you okay?"

We were all a little bit rougher in those last few days. Like animals who'd picked up on the scent of a predator—jumping at shadows, tossing with restless sleep.

"I'm fine." I steadied myself with a flush, holding up the arrows. "Target practice. Thought I might watch for a while and help them resupply."

He nodded vaguely, glancing back over his shoulder. "I just came from there. He's tireless, that man. I've never seen such focus."

I followed his gaze with another shiver.

Many nights I'd sat in the clearing, watching as Remy fired shot after shot. In a strange way it was almost soothing, the steady rhythm of it. *Almost* soothing. Then you saw the look in his eyes.

"I'll let you get to it," he murmured. "Enjoy."

I stepped aside to let him pass, then called out suddenly, "You know, I was surprised that you decided to come. Just considering Ella. I thought...I thought maybe you'd decide to stay."

He paused on the trail, then slowly turned around to face me.

"Until this is over I can't move forward, can't move on with my life." His eyes drifted down towards the valley. "I need to see for myself that Arabella's gone. Then maybe..."

I watched with a little smile, thinking of the same red-haired girl.

"And if she is?" I prompted gently. "If she was lost in the fire?"

He startled a little, snapping back to the present.

"Then I'll knock Zadie unconscious, throw her over my shoulder, and run for the hills." He flashed a lovely smile. "But good luck to the rest of you."

I laughed in spite of myself as he saluted and vanished into the trees, leaving me to head in the opposite direction. If only I'd gone a little faster. If only I hadn't stopped to talk—

"Elise?"

My heart jumped and I almost called out for Demetrius to come back. Anything to avoid having this exact conversation. Anything to avoid the inevitable moment when I'd turn around.

"I don't mean to keep you," he said quietly, "only to speak for a moment. I know you like to spend these evenings with your friends."

I stared hard at the trees, then slowly rotated around.

"My *friends* are training themselves to kill people, after being repeatedly raped by your *friends* at the palace. Other soldiers, members of the court...there was no real difference."

I took a step closer, staring right into his eyes. "So, yes—we do prefer to spend our time together. *Alone.*"

His face tightened, but he held my gaze.

"There were many in the guards who took advantage of the captives," he said softly. "I don't deny that. But you must believe that none of the men with me ever had any part."

I raised an eyebrow, but said nothing.

In truth, I didn't suspect any of the soldiers. After all, many of them were captives themselves. Only, they'd been given weapons instead of being claimed.

But that was the point. None of them chose it.

"Good talk—"

His hand flashed out as I started to walk away, catching hold of my arm. "Cricket—"

"Don't call me that," I hissed, yanking free. "And don't touch me. As you pointed out, my friends are just a scream away. And one of them is a damn good shot."

A strained silence fell between us as his hand dropped back to his side.

"I understand that you're angry," he murmured. "You lost your father over a handful of grain. But what would you have had me do, Elise? What choice did I have?"

I shook my head in astonishment, fingers curling into tight fists.

"What choice did *you* have?" I echoed faintly. "You could have chosen *not* to join the ranks of our oppressors! The same people who kidnapped your daughter and delivered her to a stranger's bed! You could have shown even a *shred* of dignity! Stood up for something greater than yourself!"

My ears were ringing, my heart pounding. And for the life of me, I couldn't understand the look on my father's face. He stood there in stunned silence, shaking his head.

"Is that what you think?" he finally managed. "That my choice was enlistment or death?"

When I offered nothing but a cold stare, his eyes softened with a sad smile.

"It wasn't my life they threatened, cricket. It was your mother's and yours."

My lips parted, but I couldn't make a sound. A part of me wanted to reject it. I'd hated him for so long. Blamed him for every day I went hungry, for every night I cried myself to sleep.

He was an easy villain and no one tried to stop me. Yet I remembered what Matthew had said about the troops stationed near the palace, how they had families to tether them behind.

"Is that the truth?" I whispered. "You made that choice...for us?"

He took a step closer. He lifted a hand to my face.

That's when the first scream rang through the trees.

WE RAN THROUGH THE forest together, my father and I.

One of his hands was on my wrist, the other on his sword. I heard quick footsteps as the others fell in stride alongside us, no idea what to expect when we broke through the trees.

Holy hell...

It was a fight, sure enough. But the fight was already over.

Our entire group slid to a collective stop at the edge of the valley, staring in astonishment at the fallen bodies and fractured spears littered across the moonlit grass. There seemed no end to the destruction—it stretched as far as the eye could see. But there were more people still standing than the ones who had fallen. People whose eyes found us at the same time.

"Who is it?" Zadie whispered, appearing suddenly beside me. "What's happened?"

There was a terrifying moment when the two sides stared at each other and all was quiet.

Then a man stepped forward, eyes twinkling through a tangle of golden hair.

"It's about time you showed up."

Chapter 15

"——Which is when those left saw the remains of the company at the station and decided to head to the valley ourselves, on the off chance that any of you had survived the flood. That's when we ran into the group you'd sent to Costan. There was another coming from Sackville as well—"

Jasper hadn't stopped talking since we found him in the valley. Perhaps it was the lingering adrenaline from the fight. Perhaps he was simply thrilled to find us alive.

"At any rate, I elected myself leader—which seemed like a great idea at the time—but then we got close enough to see the palace itself and I decided to rethink that promotion. Unfortunately, in *getting* close enough a few of the patrolling companies had seen us as well, which is when they decided to smite us once and for all. Never could they have guessed we would TRIUMPH—"

He raised his voice to a deafening cheer from the crowd.

"—which I suppose makes me a *brilliant* leader after all."

The story ended abruptly, leaving us blinking in a daze.

"Have you got any food?" he added suddenly. "I'm starving."

If it wasn't so terribly serious, I might have laughed.

After the flood in the mountains, we'd been forced to abandon the idea of reuniting with the others. After discovering the soldiers had captured and slaughtered two of the remaining groups, it was an unspoken assumption that none of the rest had survived. The men of Nimoa were too far away to help—blockading supplies and battling the queen's navy on the high seas. The rest of the provinces were isolated and waiting for aid that would never come.

It was the reason my plan was so imperative. The same reason Will had shouted Zadie down by the fire. We no longer had the numbers. We no longer stood a chance of beating them in fight.

...until now.

"I was serious about the food," Jasper prompted. "Battle is hungry work."

When none of us had the sense to move, he dropped the sword he was holding onto the grass and made his way to the nearest person, pulling the bag from his shoulder and peering inside.

He froze with a strange expression, then slowly raised his gaze. "I don't think you understand how this works..."

FOR THE NEXT FEW HOURS, the force from Nimoa rested and replenished while the rest of us stole like ghosts across the battle-field—picking up any usable weapons we could find. The sailors who survived the shipwreck were catching Jasper up on everything that had happened since we left, and by the time we returned he was in a slightly different state of mind.

"Clarify this for me," he demanded the second I stepped into sight. "There is a girl among you who actually *created* the plague that swept across the land?"

In my periphery, Jane stepped discreetly behind Will.

"Yes," I replied calmly, staring into his eyes.

He took a second to absorb this, seemed to decide it was too great a thing to process on the fly, and moved swiftly past it—delving into the logistics instead.

"And you aim to slip inside the palace and infect the court itself? Infect the soldiers? And just hope they get sick enough to *very quickly* die?"

It was impossible to miss the sarcasm, but in this part, at least, I was certain.

"It *will* be quick," I assured him, just as Jane had assured me. "After being heavily diluted, after weeks of travel, it still managed to bring a swift death to the people in the realm. Only a handful of people lingered, most died within the hour. This will be much stronger than that."

He nodded slowly, looking me up and down.

"And you're going yourself?" His handsome face sobered with a hint of respect before he flashed a mischievous smile once again. "How does your boyfriend feel about that?"

Will ground his teeth and prayed for patience, while I smiled in return.

"My *fiancé* wasn't thrilled...but he understands."

"Or you could always do it," Will suggested sweetly. "Still want to be king?"

Jasper laughed softly, glancing back over the battlefield. The adrenaline had long since faded, and he no longer saw a mass of bodies. He was picking out individual faces. The smile faded into something unexpectedly thoughtful as his eyes lifted past the castle towards the sea.

"...I want to go home."

There was a murmur of assent from the crowd of people behind him. People of all ages, from all places. United for a single purpose, if only for a time.

I nodded silently, gazing up towards those gilded towers.

"Tomorrow night, we'll slip inside the—"

"Tomorrow?" he interrupted. "I'm afraid not, love. They have *seen* us now." One hand pointed blindly back to the palace. "If you think they're going to wait another full day, you're out of your pretty little mind. At dawn, those gates will open back up. Anything you have planned, any suicidal missions to unleash some deadly disease...you'll have to do it before then."

THE GOODBYES WERE QUICK and brutal, mostly because no one actually let themselves say goodbye. They settled for stiff hugs, comical threats, and secret tears they thought no one could see.

Zadie kissed my cheek and begged to go with me. Demetrius pulled her back after giving me a silent nod. Isabelle muttered something unintelligible then shocked me with a sudden embrace, while my father stood silently behind them—tracing every movement with his eyes.

"You'll return," he said quietly when our gazes locked. "You'll return...and then we can start again."

I stared at him a moment, then nodded. "I'd like that very much."

In the end, there were only two.

"We're coming with you," Will said before I could open my mouth. "Just until you get to the trees. We'll wait for you there." He paused a moment. "And then you *will* come back."

Remy nodded firmly beside him, white knuckles gripping his bow.

It was an unnecessary risk. One that I would have tried to talk them out of if we'd been given more time. But the moment was upon us. There was no more time left to lose.

"...then let's go."

The four of us left the others behind, darting quickly across the battlefield as the moonlight clung to the tops of the nearby trees. The smell was overwhelming. It was something I'd never considered until that moment, but the air hung heavy with the stench of blood and death.

And tomorrow, there will be more.

By the time we reached the small patch of trees that provided a barrier between the palace and the village, we could already hear sounds coming from both. Jasper was right, the royal army had no intention of waiting another day before striking back. Already they were rallying the rest of their forces to march at full strength down from the palace to strike back.

"This is as far as you go," I said suddenly, turning around to face the men.

If I hadn't said anything, I had no doubt that they would have continued right along beside me. Hoping I wouldn't notice that they'd ventured into the palace as well.

Remy's eyes tightened with worry, but he took a step back. Will stepped forward instead, gently lifting my chin and leaning down with a kiss.

"This is where I'll be waiting," he said softly, taking the pack off his arm and slipping it over mine instead. "Do you hear me? I'll be waiting right here when you come back."

I forced a smile, trying very hard not to cry.

"When I come back," I echoed.

And that was it.

Without another word Jane and I left them standing in the shadows, heading once more up the same dusty pathway we'd been brought so long ago.

My first thought was to be frightened by all the commotion, but I quickly realized it worked in our favor. The once-tranquil courtyards and gardens were in such a state of disarray no one looked twice at the two hooded servant girls slipping past the iron gate.

Once we got inside, things were even more hectic.

The lords and ladies of the court fluttered past like frightened birds, their bright cloaks and dresses trailing behind them. Servants followed close behind like well-trained shadows, and scores of troops clattered down the hallways, their heavy boots slipping on the marble floor.

It was easy to be invisible. It was also a *massive* problem.

"Where am I supposed to dump the vials?" Jane hissed, fingers clenched around my arm.

The plan had been to pour it into the food supply—deliver it straight to the kitchens, who would deliver it straight to the barracks. The soldiers didn't eat with the rest of the court; it would be simple enough to make sure the sickness was contained with them.

But if those soldiers were already on the move...?

"The oil," I breathed, catching the scent of it as they marched by.

She stared up at me with wide, frightened eyes.

"What?"

Glancing around, I pulled her into a side corridor.

"They're gearing up for battle—most of them are heading to the barracks right now. Get whatever remains of the vials and pour it into the oil. They'll rub it all over their armor, use it to polish their blades. They'll be covered before they even leave the palace."

She nodded quickly, still clinging to my arm.

"And what about you?"

I clutched the strap on my shoulder.

"My part is unchanged. The enemy will be coming out to meet us. But all the servants, all the captives—everyone who was not born to this palace will be locked inside."

So that palace shall be made safe for them.

She nodded again, then paled in sudden fear.

"So...this is where we part ways."

I squeezed her hand, extracting myself at the same time. "You get the poison, I'll get the cure. We'll meet back at the gate."

There was a stricken pause.

"...and if we're captured?"

I flashed a tight smile, backing away.

"Then it's been a pleasure, Jane."

A door opened from the gardens and a crowd of people swept between us. I melted quickly against the wall, bowing my head as the servants did. By the time it cleared, the girl was already gone.

I'D NEVER FORGET THE first time I saw to the grotto. It was like stepping into a different world. A place of sensation and whimsy. One that existed half in the imagination and was only partly real. No matter how often I'd returned, that dreamlike quality had struck me every time.

I felt it again the second I opened the door. Only this time, the once-bustling chamber had been deserted and I found myself very much alone.

That's perfect, I thought, clutching the strap of my bag. *Just dump this in the water and get out of here before anyone is the wiser.*

In a rush of speed I flew across the slick stone, pulling the pack off my shoulders at the same time. It was huge, but feather-light. Filled with the same flowers that had made Jasper question our sanity just a short while ago. Without stopping to think, I ripped back the cover and shook the entire thing into the pool of heated water on the other side of the room.

The effect was instantaneous.

Crimson petals swirled into the water like a wave of blood, sending up thick clouds of aromatic steam. I pulled in a deep breath, fanning the embers to make it even hotter, then froze in sudden panic as a familiar voice rang out across the stone.

"Is someone there?"

My eyes widened with horror as I slowly pushed to my feet. A moment later, those swirling clouds of steam parted and I saw Rowan standing on the other side.

So much had happened, yet he looked exactly as I remembered. A lean slice of a man, with gracefully squared shoulders and a perpetual over-animation that glittered in his eyes.

Those eyes were on me now, wide and blank.

"...Elise?"

Anyone else I would have stampeded over. Stuck them before they could call out. Maybe even stab them with the knife Will had tucked carefully into my pocket. Anyone else.

Why did it have to be you?

"Why are you here?" he asked in that strange, flat voice. "If they catch you..." He trailed off, staring at the perfumed marsh that had transformed the pool. "...what have you done?"

Footsteps pounded outside the door. At any moment I could be discovered.

"I don't—" I took a step forward, then stopped suddenly. Would he try to stop me? The man was much stronger than I was. If nothing else, he could simply shout for the guards. I sucked in another breath, then stared up at him—willing him to understand. "That really was a beautiful dress you made for my wedding...but you see why I couldn't wear it?"

He stared back in absolute silence. Poised on the edge of a knife.

Then very slowly, he nodded.

Thank you.

I ran past him without another word, pausing only to leap onto my toes and press a parting kiss into the hollow of his cheek. Not until I reached the door did I turn back around.

"Leave this open."

That was the last I ever saw of him, frozen in the billowing clouds of steam.

IF THE PALACE WAS HECTIC before I'd slipped into the grotto, it was in complete chaos by the time I slipped back out. Perhaps it was a lack of faith in their own chances. Perhaps too many of them had been singed by the fire. More likely, whoever remained at court simply wanted to watch.

The second I stepped into the main corridor, I was knocked backwards by a swarm of people who didn't even pause to look back. I peeled myself slowly away from the wall, imagining I could already smell the scent of lissium seeping up through the walls, then let out a stifled shriek when a gloved hand clamped suddenly upon my shoulder.

"You—girl."

I went perfectly rigid as the soldier dragged me forward. My lungs had frozen. My heart was racing. My eyes stayed carefully on the floor.

Is it over already? Did he see who I was?

"These need to be taken to the queen's chamber."

A second later, a bundle of linens smacked into my chest. By the time my arms curled up around them, the man and those he'd been walking with had already left.

I stared after them incredulously, then looked down at the clothes.

The queen...?

Only then did I realize how few people actually remained at the palace. The usually tidy halls were un-swept and disheveled. The portraits on the walls looked down disapprovingly. The staff had been so greatly reduced that the queen's own linens had been thrust into the hands of a random girl.

Get rid of it. Then go meet Jane.

My arms rose to do exactly that—to toss it into a corner somewhere then flood out in a rush with the others, keep that hood pulled tight around me. My friends were waiting in the field.

But my gaze rose as well, fixing on the ceiling like I could see the towers above.

If I can kill her now...

I was gone a second later, flying in the opposite direction with my fingers clenched tightly on the laundry. Feeling the slap of that little dagger with every racing step.

THE LOWER LEVELS OF the palace were a circus, but that elusive upper wing, reserved for the greatest of all royalty, was eerily calm. The second I stepped off that winding stairway I froze in the middle of an abandoned corridor, every panting breath echoing noisily off the walls.

The last time I was here...

The last time I was there had been with Remy, Zadie, and Will. We'd just attacked two of my guards. We'd just locked Eric's in my chamber. They had been just seconds away from discovering his body on the bathroom floor. I couldn't remember if we'd heard them shout.

Get to the queen.

My other senses had abandoned me, leaving me to be guided solely by that exasperated voice echoing inside my head. If I was going to attempt this, speed was the key.

If it didn't work, the others would still have time to get back across the field before the troops burst through those gates. There would be time enough for a scuffle between Remy and Will.

Time enough for one to drag the other away.

Eric and I had resided in the uppermost towers of the palace, but the queen's chambers were at the very top. I ghosted up the stairways like a wayward spirit, keeping my eyes always locked upon the next door, melting against the walls whenever I was startled by my own breath.

By the time I reached the room I desired, I was winded and panting. But still the halls were empty. No servants bustling to make things tidy, no guards stationed outside the door.

If there aren't guards, the queen must be elsewhere.

That's what the voice told me. But I'd already come this far.

With an abundance of caution I pushed the door open, peering inside. Thick tapers had been lit, just like the last time I'd been summoned. Their flames cast dancing shadows on the walls.

But the room itself was empty.

Go. Back.

At this point, there was no reason for me to linger. It had been a fool's errand from the start. But I found myself slipping inside, shutting the door behind me, drawn to the very place I'd been running from all this time.

There was a box beside the window, very similar to the one the queen had given to me. In all likelihood, it was the very same one—the crown she'd so frightfully offered. The bedding was neatly folded, but the door to the balcony had been left ajar. Had she really stood there like I'd imagined? Two queens staring across a long and checkered board.

I took a step closer, then stopped at the faint tinkling of glass.

My eyes widened as they fell upon the crystal tower in the corner. Icicles, Will had called it, having been to the room himself. The queen's lethal poisons, stirring faintly in the breeze.

I'd never know exactly why I did it. We'd already released the cursed sickness, the game had already been played and lost—unbeknownst to the people still hurrying down the halls. The people of the court had already felt its presence. No matter how closely the secret had been guarded, the plague had been brewed within the palace, leeching silently through the gilded walls. Killing the men assigned to guard it. Changing the little girl toiling in her cell. Stealing the souls of the lords and ladies feasting cheerfully above, but it stole something else from them as well.

This is why they can't have children, I realized suddenly.

They might rule in unchallenged freedom, but it had come at a heavy cost.

A noise echoed from somewhere in the distant courtyard. Just as my friends were marching across the tiny valley, the palace was preparing itself as well.

If you don't get back now, there won't be time.

That voice was back again. This time I listened. But at the last possible moment, I doubled back and lifted my hand to that sparkling tower of glass. Even knowing the death each vial held inside, there was still something coldly beautiful about it—much like the queen herself.

I stared another moment, oddly transfixed, then in a moment I could never explain I took a random slice from the middle, paced to the box beside the window, and poured the contents over the crown. It ran like water over the diamond sides, vanishing before it touched the velvet padding.

I threw the vial onto the balcony and flew towards the door in the same instant, pausing only when I noticed the suit of armor standing alongside the bed. Men's armor. Nothing the queen would ever wear. I froze mid-step, staring in silence, then my lips parted with silent understanding.

Eric.

The sounds from the palace faded, as if the rest of the world had been put on pause.

I took a step closer, touching the tips of my fingers to the curved metal. It had been perfectly erected and positioned, just waiting for the vibrant young man to step inside. A host of tears blurred my eyes as I reached into the folds of my robe and pulled out a stray flower, the one Will had insisted I keep on my person just in case. It twirled lightly in my fingers, then I tucked it inside the metal collar as one might leave a bloom upon a grave.

A silent memorial. A silent goodbye.

Then I flew into the hallway, never to set foot in the room again.

IT TOOK A WHILE TO reach the base of the palace. The entire way down those winding stairwells, I expected to hear a shout of discovery—realizing that either Jane or I had failed. But there was nothing but a frantic tide of people when I stepped onto the ground floor.

As I'd suspected, the servants and captives had been ordered to stay within the palace—eternal prisoners of those gilded walls. But the rest of the court and soldiers had already gathered in the outer courtyards. The soldiers were assembling in the grounds behind them, waiting to depart.

Jane...where is Jane...?

At this point, I hadn't expected to find her. We'd given ourselves a strict time-table for such activities and, needless to say, I'd completely abandoned my part. I was therefore stunned when a slender hand shot to catch mine as I made my way beneath the iron gate.

"Elise!"

A whisper hissed in my ear and I whirled in shock to see her standing there—flushed and scared, yet a great deal calmer than she'd been before.

"You stayed," I gasped, stepping aside to avoid the stampede. "I didn't think—"

"You're my friend," she said shortly, dragging me towards the door. "Besides, I was afraid to slip through the gate by myself."

I laughed breathlessly, then hurried along with her. Staying carefully concealed in the crowd of people before slipping away at the last second and heading back towards the trees.

Even from so far a distance, I could hear the sound of frantic voices—two young men trying to reason with one another inside the cluster of trees. Those voices stopped the second they saw us coming. Will took a step forward, gasping with relief as he reached out a trembling hand.

Then all at once something went wrong.

I felt the shadow just as I saw it register on Will's face. That breathless smile had been replaced with a look of sheer terror as his eyes drifted past my shoulder to something just behind.

My heart stuttered to a stop. I knew who was behind me.

I turned right as he grabbed me, staring up into those wicked eyes.

"Hello again, beauty. Still making good choices?"

Chapter 16

The commander lifted me in the air just as Jane stumbled back with a scream. Will and Remy raced forward at the same time, but they froze when he pulled out a blade.

"One more step and she dies."

Calm words, but no one doubted them. The board and all its pieces froze, hovering in suspension, waiting to see what would happen next.

It was a smile.

"I had wondered if you'd make it this far," he murmured, running the tip of the knife along my jaw. "I was beginning to lose hope."

Hope.

"You wanted me to," I answered through clenched teeth, trying not to flinch as that blade caressed my skin. "The same way you wanted Eric to fall in love with me. You positioned the whole thing perfectly, did everything in your power to make it happen. Why?"

I'd expected a denial, even to the end. But the man threw back his head with a burst of laughter, unheard by the frenzied crowd in the palace above.

"Why does a man do anything?" he replied, still chuckling. "Why does he get himself up every morning? Why does he lift his eyes to the sun?"

He pointed a blind finger to the palace behind him, raising it all the way to the top.

"*That's* why. I wanted to be there. I deserved to be there. With the prince, such a thing might have been possible. But never with the queen."

Even through the terror, even knowing I was about to die...I still couldn't understand.

"With Eric—"

"The prince was a man of the people, strangely enough." His eyes glittered in the fading moonlight as they swept over the rest. "He fought alongside them—rode at the very front. The men all feared him, but he had their respect. I believe he respected them as well. In his own way."

I thrashed violently in his arms, feeling the punishing sting of the knife.

"It was for a promotion?" I hissed, seething with rage. "This whole thing—the reason you took me from my home in Midlark. That was all to get you closer to the throne?!"

He shrugged, like such things were always so simple. "You gentled him, bettered him. Made him think about things in a way he hadn't done before. His mother is set in her ways—only those of the royal bloodline will ever be permitted a place at court. But the prince...he might have changed all that."

His grip tightened.

"Not that it matters anymore."

Time's up.

I pulled in a silent breath, freezing to perfect stillness as I dangled from his hand. His eyes swept over me, head to toe, then a strangely regretful expression settled upon his face.

"It could have been so much different, beauty." He slid the blade lower, balancing on the soft skin of my throat. "I thought you were the one—"

He jerked suddenly, as though he'd stepped on something sharp. A look of confusion washed over him before his eyes drifted lower...to the arrow sticking out of his chest.

I dropped to the ground a moment later, stumbling backwards across the grass. Then I fell into Will's arms. Remy was standing tall beside him, the bow still raised to his chin.

"*...you.*"

The commander's eyes widened in astonishment, then a wild frenzy took hold. He charged forward in what felt like slow motion, barreling towards the lovely man holding the bow. The mere sight of it was enough to inspire nightmares, but amidst the chaos Remy was strangely calm.

He froze for only a moment, an involuntary stilling as the memories rushed over him in a way. Then he pulled another arrow from the quiver and drew it back, fitting it beneath his chin.

One after another, they were fired into the commander. Each one burying deep inside the man's body, until there was only one left. That manic charge had halted. He gasped and fell to his knees.

Remy tossed the bow aside and walked forward, holding that final arrow loose between his hands. There was no speech or final condemnation, nothing but a silent moment as he stared down into those fading eyes. One hand curled around the man's head, tilting it skyward.

The other buried that final arrowhead in his mouth.

DAWN WAS BREAKING.

The first streaks of a new sunrise spread above us as my friends and I sprinted back across the field. The commander's death had gone unnoticed. I supposed someone would find him later beneath the trees. The rest of the army had rallied without him, marching slowly to the gates.

We reached the others just as they creaked open behind us. I heard it all the way across the grass. A faint vibration stole through the ground, then we turned as one to see them gathering below the walls of the palace. The entire royal army...with the queen herself standing at the front.

For a fleeting moment, there wasn't a whisper of sound. Both sides stared at each other in silence, sweeping over all those familiar faces they used to know so well.

The queen drew my instant attention—standing like a statue in the center, looking exactly as I'd pictured her all this time. A fitted gown of black satin, ice-blonde hair spilling down the front. I stared in a kind of trance, like I was back in the mountains still dreaming, then my eyes drifted in astonishment to the woman standing by her side.

So the Lady Rosalynd had not been killed in the fire as was reported—she'd been maimed by it instead. Her once-flawless face was scarred and disfigured, half-hidden behind a heavy veil that did nothing to mask her vicious snarl. The lords and ladies of the palace were standing alongside her, no intention of fighting—surrounded by their host of soldiers, they were content to be mere spectators.

Gathering as though it was another form of entertainment. Come to watch our death.

There were people I'd dined with, people I'd danced with, people who'd congratulated me on my upcoming nuptials as twinkling lanterns swished in the trees. More people than I'd expected, but many were missing as well. The count and countess. Arabella Noiselle was nowhere in sight.

But that wasn't the only surprise in the crowd.

"Come here, my darling. You've yet to see your bride."

My mouth fell open.

...what?

It seemed impossible that the queen's soft voice might carry so far, but I heard every word with perfect clarity. The crowed parted in silence. A tall man was cutting through.

I watched with growing confusion...then my heart froze in my chest.

Eric.

There he was, tall and handsome, looking just the way I remembered. Just the way I saw him each night in my dreams. It was as though he'd stepped out of one of those portraits—each line was sculpted to perfection, the flawless image of a prince breathed suddenly to life.

But...how?

"Rejoice, my darling! Your beloved is alive!" The queen's dark eyes glittered in the golden sunrise, no light in them at all. "In spite of your most sincere efforts..."

There was movement in the crowd behind me, a ripple of terror at the sight of the two monarchs standing side by side.

The queen noted it with a smile. Eric only had eyes for me.

"Hello, my love."

I let out a painful gasp, as though he'd stabbed me with a blade. My eyes welled up with tears, blurring the rest of them, but the image of the prince remained impossibly clear.

"How is this happening?" I whispered. "How are you here?"

He couldn't have heard me. But he seemed to hear me all the same. His lips parted with a strange expression, as though to ask a different question, but his mother answered for us both.

"You foolish children," she murmured, eyes sweeping down the line. "You thrust a sword straight into him, striking down the prince of this land. But even in death, you still feared him. You couldn't stand to be in the same room as his body. You didn't even check his pulse."

I was vaguely aware she was still talking, but I couldn't tear my eyes away from his face. A silent connection still burned between us. Impossible to turn away from, impossible to break.

"Eric—"

"You will not speak to him!" the queen commanded, those painted lips pulled back in a snarl. "You will not dare to speak his name!"

To my own astonishment, I didn't. I stared at him instead—seeing him not as he stood in front of me, rigid and unsmiling, bedecked in the armor I'd mistaken as a memorial propped up beside the bed. But as the boy who'd laughed with me in the stables, who'd walked with me in the garden, who'd whispered promises of the future and pressed a gentle kiss to my lips. My eyes held his across all that distance before drifting down to the crimson flower still tucked in his lapel.

"So close you came," the queen murmured softly. "So many people you've gathered...and for what? Look at where you are standing! What chance do you think you have?"

At that precise moment, I was thinking the same thing.

Staring at an army that looked far greater and far healthier than I'd imagined. Staring at a man to whom I'd been promised...risen from the dead. Whatever defeat I felt she must have seen it, because another cold smile spread across her face.

"You silly girl...we offered you a crown."

A crown.

The trance broke, my eyes blinked clear. It was then I realized what I should have seen from the beginning. A sight that had become so bizarrely ordinary I no longer gave it any thought.

The queen was wearing a crown.

"Hold steady."

I spoke not to her, but to the people on my own side. The crowd around me tightened, hands gripping white upon their stolen blades. The royal forces shifted in response, their heavy armor hissing quietly beneath the sun. The queen took a step forward, lifting a blade—

—then stumbled.

It was a crack in the stillness. That chilling moment at the breach of a dam before all that caged water came spilling forth.

"You gave me a crown," I answered, watching as she raised a trembling hand to her face. It came away wet, stained with royal blood. "I thought I should give you one in return."

A wretched cry tore from her lips, even as she tore off the diamonds and hurled them to the ground. But it was too late to save her. The damage was already done.

"KILL THEM!"

She was dead a moment later. She was dead before she hit the ground.

In a mass of metal and confusion, the soldiers around her raced forward—only to stumble into the grass. The queen's poison worked faster than any plague, but all morning long they'd been gripping those weapons, working the sickness deeper and deeper into their skin.

It was a terrible sight to behold, but I watched it all the same.

They were dying faster than they were running—throwing themselves desperately towards us before careening headfirst into the grass. A few of them managed to get further than the others, few enough that they were shot down by our archers before they made it to the line. But the ground behind them was strewn with the writhing bodies of their comrades.

And the darkness didn't stop there.

I watched in silence as the men and woman of the court—still dazzling in all their gems and finery—began to splinter at the seams. It started slowly. With a sudden cough, a look of confusion, a trembling hand raised to a fevered brow. Then all delusions vanished and they screamed in earnest, racing back to the safety of the palace, falling like wilted butterflies upon the marble steps.

Jane had said that death would come in minutes, as though they'd sipped from the deadly chalice. But it seemed much faster than that. The little valley, once so pristine and peaceful, turned into a massive open grave, claiming the bodies of all those who stood upon it.

...until only one was left.

While the rest of them had flown into chaos, a writhing mass of flailing limbs, the prince had gone very still. He watched them die in silence, staring with a look of complete bewilderment, only to lift his eyes and see the rest of the realm standing in front of him, each one holding a cluster of red flowers to their face. He stared a few seconds without moving, then took the one from his lapel.

That silence gave way to sudden understanding, too surprised to make room for anything else. It twirled lightly between his fingers before his gaze drifted past me, landing upon Jane.

"So you finally did it," he murmured, still holding the petals. "You finally found peace."

She nodded in silence, quiet tears slipping down her face.

He stared back at her, then nodded abruptly—those dark eyes shining as they swept across his men. So loud they'd been, just a few moment earlier. Now everything was quiet and still.

"I didn't know about the plague," he said plainly, turning those eyes back to me. "I don't think Jane knew either. We talked for hours, she and I. Talked about everything…but I never knew why she'd been brought there. My mother didn't tell me until years after…"

He trailed into silence, looking down at his mother for the first time.

I didn't know what to say to him. At this point, I didn't know what could be done. The battle had been won and lost. All that remained was a single man standing in front of a united realm.

…holding a tiny flower instead of a blade.

His eyes swept between me and Will, lingering a moment on our entwined hands, softening almost wistfully. "I guess the better man won."

He took a step closer and a thousand swords rose into the air.

If they charged, there would be no stopping them. If they charged, I had no right to call them back. Yet standing there, staring across the bloodied grass, I wanted nothing more than to throw myself straight into their path.

"Wait!" I screamed as they started to surge forward.

A thousand people paused before me, but I had eyes for only one man.

"I'm sorry," I blurted, tears spilling down my face. "Forgive me?"

His eyes held mine for a long moment, staring with an expression I'd never forget. Then he lifted the flower to his lips, kissing it softly then tossing it to the ground.

"Elise, there is nothing to forgive."

The army surged forward. Then I could see him no more.

Epilogue

The wedding was exactly how I'd dreamed it, all those years ago. Only this time, there were a few changes. This time, I wore a simple dress.

It billowed around me as I floated down the aisle, over a sea of violet petals that had been spread across the ground that morning. They scented the air gently, mixing with the ocean breeze.

Radiant faces smiled from every direction. All my friends gathered in the same place. Remy was sitting in front with Isabelle. Zadie, Demetrius, and Ella were sitting right alongside. My parents were there as well, standing not together but not very far apart.

I stared for only a moment before lifting my eyes to something further. The man waiting for me at the end of the aisle. His eyes twinkling with a secret smile.

I SMILED AT THE MEMORY, hand resting on my belly.

I'm pregnant now. Remy encouraged me to write the story down, every single bit of it, so that I'd always remember. Will hopes it's a little girl, but I know it's a boy. A boy born to hope and freedom. A light shining in the darkness, when all other lights had gone out.

I think I'll name him Matthew.

THE END

Note from W.J. May

I hope you enjoyed the Royal Factions series. While this story is fantasy fiction, there is a part of real life to it. Child trafficking affects every country in the world. It doesn't just involve trafficking for sex, but also forced marriage, forced labor, domestic servitude, child soldiers, and so much more. Girls and boys are both vulnerable. It needs to stop. We, the world, can do better. It is our God-given duty to protect.

If you suspect someone is a victim of trafficking, contact the National Human Trafficking Resource Center[1] (https://humantraffickinghotline.org/) at 1-800-373-7888. The confidential hotline is open 24 hours a day, every day, and helps identify, protect and serve victims of trafficking.

---

1. *https://humantraffickinghotline.org/*

I wasn't as strong or fast as others in my village. If we were being selected for breeding purposes, I didn't have much to offer by means of that. I was smart, but not particularly well educated. I was kind, but no one in the provinces or the capital placed any value in that.

But ever since I was a child, people had told me I was beautiful.

A waste—they called it.

THE PRICE FOR
PEACE
USA TODAY BESTSELLING AUTHOR
W.J. MAY
THE ROYAL FACTIONS SERIES

THE PRICE FOR
PEACE
USA TODAY BESTSELLING AUTHOR
W.J. MAY
THE ROYAL FACTIONS SERIES

"I feel like I'm running too fast," I whispered. "Heading towards something terrible. And I can't stop it. I can't make it stop."

Royal Factions

The Price for Peace – Book 1
The Cost for Surviving – Book 2
The Punishment for Deception – Book 3
Faking Perfection – Book 4
The Most Cherished – Book 5
The Strength to Endure – Book 6

THE
ROYAL
FACTIONS
SERIES

The Queen's Alpha Series

Eternal
Everlasting
Unceasing
Evermore
Forever
Boundless
Prophecy
Protected
Foretelling
Revelation
Betrayal
Resolved

The Omega Queen Series

Discipline
Bravery
Courage
Conquer
Strength
Validation

Find W.J. May

Website:
http://www.wanitamay.yolasite.com
Facebook:
https://www.facebook.com/pages/Author-WJ-May-FAN-PAGE/
141170442608149
Newsletter:
SIGN UP FOR W.J. May's Newsletter to find out about new releases,
updates, cover reveals and even freebies!
http://eepurl.com/97aYf

More books by W.J. May

The Chronicles of Kerrigan

Book I - *Rae of Hope* is FREE!
Book Trailer:
http://www.youtube.com/watch?v=gILAwXxx8MU
Book II - *Dark Nebula*
Book Trailer:
http://www.youtube.com/watch?v=Ca24STi_bFM
Book III - *House of Cards*
Book IV - *Royal Tea*
Book V - *Under Fire*
Book VI - *End in Sight*
Book VII – *Hidden Darkness*
Book VIII – *Twisted Together*
Book IX – *Mark of Fate*
Book X – *Strength & Power*
Book XI – *Last One Standing*
BOOK XII – *Rae of Light*

PREQUEL –
Christmas Before the Magic

Question the Darkness
Into the Darkness
Fight the Darkness
Alone the Darkness
Lost the Darkness

SEQUEL –

Matter of Time
Time Piece
Second Chance
Glitch in Time
Our Time
Precious Time

Hidden Secrets Saga:
Download Seventh Mark part 1 For FREE
Book Trailer:
http://www.youtube.com/watch?v=Y-_vVYC1gvo

Like most teenagers, Rouge is trying to figure out who she is and what she wants to be. With little knowledge about her past, she has questions but has never tried to find the answers. Everything changes when she befriends a strangely intoxicating family. Siblings Grace and Michael, appear to have secrets which seem connected to Rouge. Her hunch is confirmed when a horrible incident occurs at an outdoor party. Rouge may be the only one who can find the answer.

An ancient journal, a Sioghra necklace and a special mark force life-altering decisions for a girl who grew up unprepared to fight for her life or others.

All secrets have a cost and Rouge's determination to find the truth can only lead to trouble...or something even more sinister.

RADIUM HALOS - THE SENSELESS SERIES
Book 1 is FREE

Everyone needs to be a hero at one point in their life.

The small town of Elliot Lake will never be the same again.

Caught in a sudden thunderstorm, Zoe, a high school senior from Elliot Lake, and five of her friends take shelter in an abandoned uranium mine. Over the next few days, Zoe's hearing sharpens drastically, beyond what any normal human being can detect. She tells her friends, only to learn that four others have an increased sense as well. Only Kieran, the new boy from Scotland, isn't affected.

Fashioning themselves into superheroes, the group tries to stop the strange occurrences happening in their little town. Muggings, break-ins, disappearances, and murder begin to hit too close to home. It leads the team to think someone knows about their secret - someone who wants them all dead.

An incredulous group of heroes. A traitor in the midst. Some dreams are written in blood.

Courage Runs Red
The Blood Red Series
Book 1 is FREE

WHAT IF COURAGE WAS your only option?

When Kallie lands a college interview with the city's new hot-shot police officer, she has no idea everything in her life is about to change. The detective is young, handsome and seems to have an unnatural ability to stop the increasing local crime rate. Detective Liam's particular interest in Kallie sends her heart and head stumbling over each other.

When a raging blood feud between vampires spills into her home, Kallie gets caught in the middle. Torn between love and family loyalty she must find the courage to fight what she fears the most and possibly risk everything, even if it means dying for those she loves.

Daughter of Darkness - Victoria
Only Death Could Stop Her Now
The Daughters of Darkness is a series of female heroines who may or may not know each other, but all have the same father, Vlad Montour. Victoria is a Hunter Vampire

Paranormal
HUNTRESS SERIES
USA TODAY BESTSELLING AUTHOR
W.J. MAY
LOOK BACK
MASTER
PERMISSION

PROPHECY SERIES
USA TODAY BESTSELLING AUTHOR
• W.J. MAY •
PROPHECY
PROPHECY
PROPHECY
• W.J. MAY •
• W.J. MAY •
• W.J. MAY •

Don't miss out!

Visit the website below and you can sign up to receive emails whenever W.J. May publishes a new book. There's no charge and no obligation.

https://books2read.com/r/B-A-SSF-NNVJB

BOOKS2READ

Connecting independent readers to independent writers.

Did you love *The Strength to Endure*? Then you should read *The Kerrigan Kids Box Set Books #1-3*[1] by W.J. May!

USA Today Bestselling author, W.J. May brings you a continuation of the international bestselling series, The Chronicles of Kerrigan! Come back and enjoy the famous characters, or step into the series right here. You won't be disappointed! Grab the first three books of the 12 book series!

<u>Book 1 - School of Potential</u>

How do you save the world, when it's already been saved?

Eighteen-year-old Aria was supposed to have it all. A tight-knit circle of friends, a loving family, and a magical tatu on her lower back that gave her every superpower under the sun. When it came to the battle between good and evil, she was ready to do her part. There was just one little problem.

---

1. https://books2read.com/u/b6K9jp

2. https://books2read.com/u/b6K9jp

...good had already won.

Trapped beneath their parents' legacy, Aria and her friends find themselves restlessly pacing the halls of Guilder University, desperate to come into their powers, desperate for whatever comes next. The months blend together, each more monotonous than the next, until one day, no different than any other, a mysterious stranger comes to school.

Determined to uncover his secrets and driven by a fierce need to prove themselves, the new gang does whatever it takes to show the rest of the world they're ready. But that readiness comes at a cost.

Will it be a price they're willing to pay?

Book 2 - Myths & Magic

It was a trial by fire...

When a vicious murder rocks the Guilder Boarding School, Aria and her friends find themselves on shaky ground. When everyone has motive, everyone's a suspect. And thanks to a public brawl with the victim, Aria Wardell was seen to have more motive than most.

While fending off a ward of accusations from both the students and the faculty alike, Aria struggles to find balance in her life amidst the shocking development of some new powers. A new group of shifters on campus raise more questions than answers, and no matter how the world is crumbling around her, she can't get a certain moonlit kiss out of her mind.

Trouble is brewing. Secrets can't stay secret for long.

Will she ever get answers? Or should some secrets be taken to the grave?

Book 3 - Kith & Kin

If you can't beat them, join them...

When yet another attack leaves the students of Guilder University looking for answers, Aria decides to take matters into her own hands. Armed with a set of powers she'd vowed never to use, she follows the clues to the killer—only to find that nothing is as it seems.

The world is changing. Alliances are shifting. And the very foundations of the supernatural community are at risk. Like it or not, people are starting to take sides.

But will Aria and her friends find themselves on the right side of the fight? Or are some sins too big to come back from?

Kerrigan Kids

Book 1 - School of Potential

Book 2 - Myths & Magic

Book 3 - Kith & Kin

Book 4 - Playing With Power

Book 5 - Line of Ancestry

Book 6 - Descent of Hope

Book 7 – Illusion of Shadows

Book 8 – Frozen by the Future

Book 9 – Guilt of My Past

Book 10 – Demise of Magic

Book 11- Rise of the Prophecy

Book 12 – Deafened by the Past

Read more at www.wjmaybooks.com.

Also by W.J. May

Bit-Lit Series
Lost Vampire
Cost of Blood
Price of Death

Blood Red Series
Courage Runs Red
The Night Watch
Marked by Courage
Forever Night
The Other Side of Fear
Blood Red Box Set Books #1-5

Daughters of Darkness: Victoria's Journey
Victoria
Huntress
Coveted (A Vampire & Paranormal Romance)
Twisted
Daughter of Darkness - Victoria - Box Set

Great Temptation Series
The Devil's Footsteps
Heaven's Command
Mortals Surrender

Hidden Secrets Saga
Seventh Mark - Part 1
Seventh Mark - Part 2
Marked By Destiny
Compelled
Fate's Intervention
Chosen Three
The Hidden Secrets Saga: The Complete Series

Kerrigan Chronicles
Stopping Time
A Passage of Time
Ticking Clock
Secrets in Time
Time in the City
Ultimate Future

Mending Magic Series
Lost Souls
Illusion of Power
Challenging the Dark

Castle of Power
Limits of Magic
Protectors of Light

Omega Queen Series
Discipline
Bravery
Courage
Conquer
Strength
Validation
Approval
Blessing
Balance

Paranormal Huntress Series
Never Look Back
Coven Master
Alpha's Permission
Blood Bonding
Oracle of Nightmares
Shadows in the Night
Paranormal Huntress BOX SET

Prophecy Series
Only the Beginning
White Winter
Secrets of Destiny

Revamped Series
Hidden
Banished
Converted

Royal Factions
The Price For Peace
The Cost for Surviving
The Punishment For Deception
Faking Perfection
The Most Cherished
The Strength to Endure

The Chronicles of Kerrigan
Rae of Hope
Dark Nebula
House of Cards
Royal Tea
Under Fire
End in Sight
Hidden Darkness
Twisted Together
Mark of Fate
Strength & Power
Last One Standing
Rae of Light
The Chronicles of Kerrigan Box Set Books # 1 - 6

The Chronicles of Kerrigan: Gabriel
Living in the Past
Present For Today
Staring at the Future

The Chronicles of Kerrigan Prequel
Christmas Before the Magic
Question the Darkness
Into the Darkness
Fight the Darkness
Alone in the Darkness
Lost in Darkness
The Chronicles of Kerrigan Prequel Series Books #1-3

The Chronicles of Kerrigan Sequel
A Matter of Time
Time Piece
Second Chance
Glitch in Time
Our Time
Precious Time

The Hidden Secrets Saga
Seventh Mark (part 1 & 2)

The Kerrigan Kids
School of Potential
Myths & Magic
Kith & Kin
Playing With Power
Line of Ancestry
Descent of Hope
Illusion of Shadows
Frozen by the Future
Guilt Of My Past
Demise of Magic
The Kerrigan Kids Box Set Books #1-3

The Queen's Alpha Series
Eternal
Everlasting
Unceasing
Evermore
Forever
Boundless
Prophecy
Protected
Foretelling
Revelation
Betrayal
Resolved
The Queen's Alpha Box Set

The Senseless Series
Radium Halos - Part 1
Radium Halos - Part 2
Nonsense
Perception
The Senseless - Box Set Books #1-4

Standalone
Shadow of Doubt (Part 1 & 2)
Five Shades of Fantasy
Zwarte Nevel
Shadow of Doubt - Part 1
Shadow of Doubt - Part 2
Four and a Half Shades of Fantasy
Dream Fighter
What Creeps in the Night
Forest of the Forbidden
Arcane Forest: A Fantasy Anthology
The First Fantasy Box Set

Watch for more at www.wjmaybooks.com.

About the Author

About W.J. May

Welcome to USA TODAY BESTSELLING author W.J. May's Page! SIGN UP for W.J. May's Newsletter to find out about new releases, updates, cover reveals and even freebies! http://eepurl.com/97aYf

Website: http://www.wjmaybooks.com

Facebook: http://www.facebook.com/pages/Author-WJ-May-FAN-PAGE/141170442608149?ref=hl *Please feel free to connect with me and share your comments. I love connecting with my readers.* W.J. May grew up in the fruit belt of Ontario. Crazy-happy childhood, she always has had a vivid imagination and loads of energy. After her father passed away in 2008, from a six-year battle with cancer (which she still believes he won the fight against), she began to write again. A passion she'd loved for years, but realized life was too short to keep putting it off. She is a writer of Young Adult, Fantasy Fiction and where ever else her little muses take her.

Read more at www.wjmaybooks.com.